RESCUE
CHRONICLES

To my grandfather,
Captain Cornelius "Con" Christopher Sullivan
(SFFD Retired), for his steady hand when I
was young. Our special relationship and his stories
of the San Francisco Fire Department at the turn
of the century are the cornerstone of this book.

And to my wife,
Annette,
who is always there for me and takes the
brunt of my guff. She knows how to put me in my
place and has been a guiding light in my life

RESCUE
CHRONICLES

Chapter One

FROM THE WEATHERED SECOND-STORY DECK BEHIND the house, a thick, frayed rope, a zip line, ran some 100 feet from a shaky anchor point, scarcely clearing a line of rosebushes, a picket fence, and a hedge at the back of Mrs. Martin's house. Perched on the railing of the deck, Luc peered out through the fog and could see only the rope. Even on a gloomy summer day like today, staying inside in front of a computer screen was not for Luc and his best friend, Jack. It wasn't in their DNA.

"Where did you get this rope?" asked Jack.

"Found it in a pile of stuff near the garbage cans by the fire station."

Jack, with question marks all over his face, thought the rope had seen better days.

"Are you sure...?"

"Don't worry, just hang on. Trust me, it works in the video." Luc was always confident before a rescue exercise.

"You mean you've never done this before?" Jack loosened his grip and started the slide away from the railing and onto the deck, thinking twice.

Luc took another appraising look at their zip-line setup. Maybe it wasn't exactly by the book, but it was close. That was good enough for him. Now he would finally be able to simulate a high-angle rescue maneuver. It would be cool to have that under his belt before summer vacation.

He looked off into the foggy distance towards where Ocean Beach should be. *Interesting perspective from here,* he thought. *How come I never tried this before?* Luc lived in the Outer Sunset District of San Francisco just south of Golden Gate Park. The fog was so dense you could hardly tell that summer vacation was only a week away. They did not call it "June gloom" for nothing; it seemed like sunshine never broke through. Luc turned back to the situation at hand and tried to calculate the distance from the weathered deck at his feet to the top of the protruding eaves of the two-story house, figuring if there were 12 feet per story with the remainder above the window and eaves adding a foot or two at the peak, that they were about 22 feet up in the air.

Luckily Mrs. Martin was not at home on Tuesday and Thursday mornings because she went to her Zumba class at the Y; Luc had heard her tell Mom. Besides, she would never find out, because the attachment at her end had been there for years. So what if the eyebolt was rusted, weathered, and bent? It had survived probably 75 years since their two post-WWII houses had been built, Luc reasoned. That bolt still clung firmly to the back wall of the house; he had checked it himself.

"I dunno, Luc," said Jack, doubt overwhelming the tone of his voice. "What if the brake doesn't work?"

"Her kids were doing this before I could walk," said Luc. "They never got in trouble or hurt, seriously." Luc checked his cell, swiping the screen to camera. "Jaaaack, smiiiile! Putting this out on Facebook, dude."

"Think we could stick to one thing at a time?" Jack replied, climbing back onto the railing and reaching for the rope.

Luc, juggling more than one thing at once, repeated the hitching instructions to Jack as they both fumbled to harness in. Luc had read all about the maneuver in the firefighters' manual his grandfather kept on the bookshelf at his house, even making a few improvements to what he could remember from the YouTube video and the zip-line trick the Martin kids had enacted a decade before. So what if they had only done it from the top of the first story? What was 12 more measly feet to a firefighter in training?

"Okay, Jack, sit up on the railing, then grab onto me once I'm set."

Jack planted his rear end on the 2-inch by 6-inch fog-soaked railing, unaware of the flaking chips of paint stuck to his butt. Luc pulled down on the taut rope, then yanked up on the makeshift harness around his chest, bringing the two together.

"Are you sure about this?" Jack repeated.

"I can control the speed by gripping harder on the rope with Mom's gardening gloves." Luc looked at Jack's face, an anticipatory grin spreading across his freckled face.

In a flash the boys were hurling downward, blind, their mouths wide open, yelling in concert and at full pitch like demented Tarzans. Within what seemed like only milliseconds, Jack's big feet had taken out Mrs. Sullivan's rosebushes, Luc and Jack had plunged through the fence together, Jack had ended up in the hedge on the other side, and Luc had continued out of control, closing his mouth just in time to fly through Mrs. Martin's open bathroom window.

Chapter Two

Luc's return trip was bumpy. As he fell back into the present tense, the sights and sounds, smells and sensations of his fire rescue experience lingered strongly.

He could feel the density of the soot on his cheeks, still hot from extended exposure to the extreme heat of the fire. Faint traces of smoke coming from his clothing brought it all back... With heart pumping and mouth dry, he had set about his task. Somehow, his own safety not the priority. By no means a game, it was him against the beast, and he was in it to win.

The walls had been blistering from within, fire racing through the bones of the building. As he moved closer to the origin, the muffled sound of the outside subsided and was replaced with the increasing crackling sound of the inferno as it ate away at everything in its path. The oaky scent of the once-hazy smoke pressurized the rooms from the ceiling and banked downward, permeating everything and everyone. The last bastion of life-saving air was then only to be found on the ground. The heat increased, coming from above, his ears beginning to burn first. Stay low! The deeper he inched forward, as if dipping his toes in a pool of icy water, the less he wanted to move.

He heard a voice. Was it a groan of life coming from beyond in the smoke? Visibility nil, Luc made out the glow through the gaseous particles. With renewed purpose he moved on, following the wall that got him to that point. Now crawling on his knees, he bumped into a lifeless body. The needle in the haystack. No time to think. Latching on as best he could, seizing the moment, he turned and dragged the victim back along the wall from where he had come.

The unrelenting clock of life continued to tick, and the fire advanced with a vengeance. His struggle paid off as he entered the safe refuge. All the pressure he had put behind him earlier was now realized as it left his body on empty, exhausted to the point no scale could weigh.

Exhilarated? Most certainly! Saving a life settled in to become a part of his being. That was what firefighters did. Fires were the context from which they rose to the challenge, like phoenixes clad in black and yellow fire-resistant gear.

All these relived sensations reached Luc's lips. In a calm, quiet voice, he croaked, "Ahh, it was a good one." He found himself savoring the aroma of the burn, wiping the black smear of ash across his face as he rubbed his reddened eyes with two filthy fists.

"Grandpa, I was there, right in the middle of the story you were telling me!"

This latest fire rescue experience back in the past was Luc's third. During the first two times he had transported back in time, he had only been allowed to participate as a rookie. The other guys had practically ignored him, and the fire captain had forbidden him from entering the fire without an escort to track his every move. This last time there had been no time to partner up. He had heard that a victim was trapped in a sector of the fire close to where he stood at the back of the old brick building, and he had not thought twice. He had just acted. And while he had not been able to save the man, Luc had retrieved the body for the man's family to have something more than ashes and bones to bury. Sadly, Doing your best is not always enough.

Before he had a second to consider entering the fire once more, he had found himself tumbling forward through time, only to land in a heap in his grandfather's living room, right in front of Grandpa, sitting just as he had before Luc had transported to the past. His grandpa had been weaving knots on his favorite fathom of rope. And he was still doing it when Luc looked up, dazed from the rapidity of the trip through time.

His grandfather smiled. He had been waiting for weeks for Luc to gain his feet, to find the confidence, some would say reckless lack of self-regard, that it took for a rookie to graduate to a rescue firefighter ready to serve in full capacity at a moment's notice.

Grandpa chuckled as he regarded his grandson. Luc Sullivan was just 13 years old, but he was already tall and lanky, indications of the man he would grow into already showing in his size 13 shoes. Half Irish, half Italian, the boy had big brown eyes framed by blond, curly hair. Grandpa Sullivan was used to peering at the boy from this angle, Luc on the floor staring up at him with wide eyes as he retold his firefighting rescue stories of the brave men who performed heroic acts. His grandson had always listened intently, occasionally breaking in with a question. It had been their favorite pastime since Luc had been about three years old. But Grandpa Sullivan had been waiting a decade to send the boy out. It had only been in the last few weeks that Luc had finally become ready to meet his destiny. Finally ready to learn from the past before he could move into the present and, ultimately, the future.

Grandpa lay down his fathom of knotting rope on the arm of the favorite old LaZBoy and put his palms on his knees as he raised up his still-strong, still-tall body and nodded at Luc, who was now sitting cross-legged on the floor, working out the tenseness of his muscles post-rescue. "Come on, Luc, I want you to meet someone."

Luc felt his heart begin to race in anticipation as Grandpa approached the mantelpiece. Surely it was too soon to go on another rescue? But Grandpa did not reach for the old-fashioned casque fire helmet; he reached instead for the stone bust of Florian.

"That's my favorite thing in your entire house, Grandpa," said Luc. "But I totally have no idea who it's supposed to be."

"That, my boy, is Florian, the patron saint of fire-fighters. He was a centurion of the first cohort elected by the Senate of Rome to command in the north. He was the Emperor Diocletian's and Diocletian's people's favorite soldier."

"Like a general?"

"Yes, a soldier firefighter, with both military duties and those of organizing an elite group of soldiers whose sole duty was to fight fires. Florian commanded a legion of men and had a well-deserved reputation for discipline but fairness. In history, Florian, who always led from the front of the battle lines, was very well thought of in Rome and in Noricum, Austria, the northernmost alpine border of the Roman Empire and his home, his birthplace."

"What happened to him?"

"Life was good. The Roman Empire was thriving. But for all soldiers, duty came first. Orders from Rome took precedence over all other interests and activities. But then Rome decided to up the ante on its relentless persecution of Christians, and Florian decided to defy the emperor's decree."

"I don't get it, why?"

"Florian had become a Christian himself; he was one with the majority of the people. He didn't want to enslave them and drive them out."

"But were the Christians a threat to Rome?"

"The emperor thought so. Likely they were not. Regardless, Florian now became one of the hunted. And since he was so well known, and a hero to boot, the emperor mandated his death."

Luc shivered. "So his guys turned against him? So they could obey the emperor?"

"Florian actually challenged his ex-comrades-in-arms to just *try* to burn him at the stake."

"Grandpa, why would he do that? He'd be killed! There were tons of them and only one of him!"

"He was first and foremost a firefighter. The threat of fire didn't faze him, Luc. And when the mob came after him, he told the crowd that the very tips of the flames that were threatening his life would actually help him ascend faster to heaven." Grandpa paused, stroking the hair of the stone figure.

"And...?" Luc pushed.

"Some of those once-loyal soldiers and firefighter comrades saw this as a premonition. They believed that Florian was already closer to the gods and that he knew something they did not. So they fled in fear. Those who remained continued to enforce the edict handed down by the emperor; they could not afford to be seen as traitors to Rome. But their new tactic was to place a millstone around Florian's neck to drown him in the River Enns."

"He didn't let them, did he? I mean, Florian didn't, did he?"

"I'm sorry to say that on that day Florian passed into the next world. And with his death the legend was born. For even though he died, Florian met his fate with the people deciding his destiny. Henceforth to this day, Florian is considered the protector of those who fight fire with water."

Luc regarded the statue. "You mean, same as you? Same as Dad?"

"Precisely. Legend also leads us to believe that the millstone that ended it for Florian now exists in amulet form and is waiting somewhere in the past for a new hero to find it."

Luc stood up straighter. "Waiting?"

"The amulet is a symbol of the virtues of Florian and his sacrifice. It is believed that when the amulet finds its proper place, either with someone special or in someplace special here in the present, it will give those who have it sovereign power when risking their lives to save others."

"I don't get it." Luc shook his head. His grandfather was speaking in tongues as far as he could understand.

"What it means, my boy, is that Florian's amulet is in limbo. And in fact, you are the one who has been charged with finding that amulet so you can continue Florian's work, firefighters' work, committing acts of heroism in the care and defense of others. And you've already been prepped with years of my storytelling." Grandpa nodded, as if to say "And that's that!"

"Wait!" cried Luc. "You mean all your stories about all those famous fires are somehow tied to my finding this amulet?"

"Now you're catching on, Luc!"

Luc frowned and stared straight ahead, processing these new connections. "So... making me study the rescue manuals and practicing knots together and talking about how different kinds of construction affect how fire travels and how fire has a life of its own... all that was leading up to this?"

"Bingo!"

"But those fires are in the past. They've already happened. How does my being there to help out change anything? How does finding the amulet help anything?"

"When you are in the service of others as a fire-fighter in the past, and when you find that amulet, you are actually preserving history. You're there kind of like an angel to make sure that events proceed as they are supposed to, so that history survives intact."

"But what happens if I—" he corrected himself— "*when* I find that amulet? Do I still have to travel back in time to all those fires?"

"Whoa, Nellie!" said Grandpa. "First things first. First, commit to your time-traveling mission and do what you're supposed to. Your vigilance, what you learn, and what you do will lead you to the amulet, I hope. What we do after that we'll deal with then."

Luc just shook his head. "Okay... but I thought you said preparation is what always saves the day in times of great danger."

"Indeed I did," agreed Grandpa. "And I hope you've been listening carefully all these years to all those stories, because preparation time is over. Now is the time for you to do what you need to do. That's what these practice trips have been all about. Don't you want to be a fire rescue captain one day?"

"You know I do, Grandpa," said Luc.

"Well, let's get on with it. I don't have all summer!"

Chapter Three

SCHOOL WAS FINALLY OUT FOR SUMMER. BUT INSTEAD of hanging out with the guys or going to Grandpa's for his first really important time travel rescue, Luc was busy sanding boards to replace the ones he and Jack had broken when they crashed through the backyard fence into Mrs. Martin's house. Then there was the nailing and the painting and... ugh. It felt endless.

Just when Luc thought he couldn't take being alone and working on the fence for one more second, Jack showed up, walking out of the foggy background with a pair of cleats tied by the laces over his shoulder.

"Hey, Jack! Save me from myself, please! And what's with the old-school, high-top cleats?"

"Dude, football of course. Didn't you get the tweet? Football tryouts are today. Look at your incoming."

Luc pulled off the cloth gloves he was wearing to protect himself from sanding splinters, pulled his phone out of his pocket, and started to scroll through his texts... and scroll... and scroll...

"Sully! You've got way too many fire rescue downloads on that phone, dude. You better delete some of that stuff or you'll never find out what's happening with us guys. 'Cause it's not like we're ever going to be hanging out to try another rescue maneuver again. My butt *still* stings from that stupid hedge."

"You didn't think it was such a bad idea up to that point," Luc interjected.

"Dude! You're *so* wrong! What was I thinking?" and here he started mimicking Luc: "...egressing from the burning building using a Telford line—whatever that means—you were harnessed in and I was totally in freefall, taking out Mrs. Martin's new hedge—thank you very fifty bucks much—while we leveled the back fence just so you could see the old lady's booty!"

"Hey!" Luc resented that. Like he wanted to see *anyone's* booty, much less Mrs. Martin's. It was not like he had *planned* to go through the window or anything. Not like he had *planned* to end up practically sitting on Mrs. Martin while she sat on the pot. He shivered. It was all too gross to remember. He looked at Jack. "What're you complaining about? You got off with paying fifty bucks. I had to pay fifty bucks *and* work my butt off here all summer till it's all fixed. So why aren't you helping me anyway?"

Jack rolled his eyes and held up his left hand. It had an ACE bandage around the palm and wrist.

"And aren't you lucky I was there? My EMT skills really came into play, like my excellent response time. I was totally at your side before shock could set in. I administered proper treatment based on the protocols I had downloaded onto my—"

"Yeah, quick response time all right," Jack interrupted. "Fastest I've ever seen you move. Dang! I would've moved fast to get out of that bathroom, too! And as far as your EMT skills go, could you read the whole chapter next time?"

"What are you talking about?"

"Let's see: I sprained my left hand—you taped up the right one. I had thorns in my butt, and I was screaming. You were checking to see if I was breathing."

"That's the new protocol: Compressions, Airway, Breathing."

"Great. If I was *screaming* don't you think maybe I was breathin' and circulatin', too?"

"Yeah, I guess so." Dude had him there, Luc thought. "Just trying to help."

"I know. It's cool, Sully. Someday you'll get it right." Jack started heading toward the streetcar stop. "Come on, let's get to tryouts."

Luc looked up at his house and at the huge pile of planks waiting to get sanded. "Where are they?"

"Tryouts are up on 25th Avenue. McCoppin Field."

"I thought they were down the street at our park, South Sunset?"

"Nope, they keep all the football equipment in the basement of the fire station across the street, locker rooms, too."

Luc had to do some quick thinking. His mom thought he was in the backyard being an obedient son and working on the fence like Tom Sawyer. If he took a streetcar all the way to 25th Avenue without permission, he could be in trouble. The rule was that he could go anywhere around the 'hood that was within earshot. McCoppin Field was definitely out of earshot. Then again, he did have an entire summer ahead of him to work on the fence. And football tryouts only came once a year...

Jack was tapping his Chucks impatiently.

The pressure to be cool was on. Luc weighed his options. If he did not go to tryouts, he would be spending all season on the sidelines or being something stupid like team water boy while all his friends played football. But if he did try out and he made it, his parents would be really proud of him, right? And he had to stop at four o'clock anyway to go visit Grandpa and take the dogs for a walk. And he *did* have all summer to fix the fence anyway...

Luc tossed down the gloves and pulled off his dad's tool belt he had been wearing to make himself feel better while working for slave wages—actually working on something he had to pay his parents to "get" to do. What was the justice in that? But he'd also never strayed away from the schoolyard, park, or outside the neighborhood without asking permission before. But, heck, he was going to be in eighth grade soon, practically high school, taking the streetcar everywhere anyway. Still, what would his mom say? And what would she do? Would she tell Dad? Was it really all that wrong? And wasn't football healthy for you, exercise and all that? All the guys were doin' it. Just then, a bunch of his friends slid in next to Jack and him.

"Hey, Sully! Okay, gang's all here," their friend Ryan said, bringing up the rear.

"Hey," another friend named Will said, "nobody said anything about cleats."

"That's just so not cool," said Alex, the youngest of the lot. "Jack's got an advantage."

Luc reached over and grabbed the cleats. "Are you serious? I bet tryouts will be over by the time those granny knots in the laces are freed up."

Jack looked at the multiple mounds of knots resembling a Rubik's Cube of sorts. The cleats looked like they were from the '80s—even the laces were all stiff with crust. They had been his dad's cleats from college.

The L Taraval streetcar approached. It was practically empty.

Luc lost his nerve. "Hey guys, I can't go. I need to be at Grandpa's by 4:00. He's expecting me."

"You'll be back by 3:45. It's just tryouts," Jack said. Everyone chimed in at once while corralling Luc onto the L. They all paid their fares and moved toward the back as the driver checked the rearview with one eye, just to see what they were all up to. *I'll deal with Mom later,* Luc thought. The fact that he already felt he'd done something wrong probably meant he had.

Luc tried to shrug off his nervousness by talking. "Last time I was on a streetcar was this past Christmas. My mom made us all go to Union Square for photos, then lunch, then the roof rides—"

"I'm on the streetcar a lot," Ryan said. "With parking being so bad, this is the best transportation for my mom to get my little sister and me to swim team practice."

"I like the way the car chugs up the track from stop to stop swaying back and forth, kinda like a roller coaster," Alex said, watching as each block slowly passed by.

"I've decided—" began Will.

Ryan cut him off. "What now, Will*is*? And by the way I'm gonna be the quarterback."

"Quarterback!" They all chimed in, each one shouting out. "I want it."

"No, I'm the one."

"Coach'll pick me for sure!"

"You throw like a girl!"

"And this girl's arm is waaaay better than your skinny little toddler-boy—"

"Did you see the TD I threw the other day?" Ryan said when the others took a bragging break. "I got the touch. I got it in the bag."

As usual they all spoke over one another, and no one got heard.

Luc was still thinking about going outside the line with his mom when the driver yelled out, "Twenty-fifth Avenue, next stop." The doors collapsed open, and they all piled out. The long streetcar slid past, and the boys crossed the street looking both ways for oncoming cars, ever aware not to trip on the streetcar tracks and look the fool in front of everyone else.

Twenty-fifth Avenue was a steep hill with the firehouse at the top. Luc recalled his grandfather teaching him why fire stations were located at the tops of hills. During the days of the horse-drawn engines, they would get quicker response times going downhill with horses, gravity being pretty practical.

The boys finally reached the top of the hill, where the old firehouse perched atop the grade as if it were keeping a vigilant eye on the district below. All the guys knew about Luc's family background going back generations with the fire service, and respect gleamed in everyone's eyes. Luc, seeing the fire hall, was reminded of his impending voyage. The Florian amulet and the responsibilities attached to any new journeys back in time was awesome. But first he wanted to test his football prowess against his friends.'

"Check out the quarterback line," Luc remarked under his breath.

"I hate to say it, but I believe three-quarters of the kids here think they're quarterbacks."

The boys stood, posturing cool, as they anxiously waited their turn.

"Alright, kid, what's your name?" the coach in charge yelled.

"Ryan."

"Can you throw?"

"I think so."

"Your turn. Hit your receiver, down and out."

Ryan moved back, set it up, and let it fly... kinda. While his arm was going forward, the ball slipped out of his hand and died in flight, nowhere close to the receiver.

"Next!" yelled the coach.

"But, but—" Ryan said.

"Sorry, kid, need to keep moving." The outcome for the rest of the guys was fairly predictable: weak. No one had bothered to warm up, and they had not played a lot of street ball or pickup games for a while. Then came

Will. All eyes focused on him as he sashayed up to the line of scrimmage, full of confidence and ready for the challenge. Will was a good athlete and could throw, too—and he knew it. Still, he was one of the guys, so they were all pulling for him. Will moved back to pass and let it fly, delivering a beauty: a spiraling bullet down the middle... No one home. No one close.

"Next!" Coach ordered.

"But, I..."

"Got to know where people are going," replied the coach. "And Will... ?"

"Yeah, Coach?"

"You're pretty good size, and I bet pretty tough and smart, too, right?"

"You bet I am."

"Well, I'm gonna put you at the next closest position to QB and that's Center."

"Center? What's with that?"

"You get to touch the ball on every down, and I need someone I can have faith in."

"Okay, cool, I think."

The wind had been knocked out of Will's sails, as Luc's grandpa would say. The rest of the tryouts did not go much better for the other boys. The good news was, they were all asked to return, each one making the first cut. Out of 200 or so kids, only half were asked back to field three teams. At least all the guys in Luc's posse were in the hunt. As they left practice, Luc looked at his phone. It was later than he thought, and he needed to get back within shouting distance of home. But he had promised to go by Grandpa's, too. He left the guys in the dust and caught the first streetcar down into the Avenues.

First stop was Grandpa's house at 42nd and Ulloa Streets.

Chapter Four

EVEN BEFORE LUC MADE IT TO THE HOUSE, GRANDPA'S dogs, Dante and Renzo, smelled him coming. The two large Rhodesian Ridgebacks, or African Lion Hounds, were big enough to scare the heck out of someone if that someone did not know that they were friendly and super smart. But they, like most animals, knew good from bad when it came to humans.

"Hey fellas, it's me, Luc!" The dogs bounded out of the house and proceeded to take down Luc while they smothered him with gooey kisses and doggy breath. Just as Luc made it to his feet, he could see Grandpa kneeling on one leg tending the rosebushes. The evident devotion to the garden was reflected in its every foot. Grandpa spoke without turning.

"Oh, there you are Luc, just in time. You know, your grandmother cherished this garden. She worked what used to be mere sand into a green, colorful oasis. She tended her family the same, come to think of it."

But before Luc could comment on his grandfather's trip into the sentimentality of his past, Grandpa said, "Would you get me the dust pan and broom? I need to tidy up a bit."

"I'll get it. Take a break." Dashing to the side of the house. Grandpa stood up, up, up, and up. Even for his age, his figure was imposing, tall and strapping.

Grandpa was a retired captain in the San Francisco Fire Department. He had been a highly respected living legend among those he trained, and those who had heard some of the stories were awed by his still-commanding presence. His given name was Cornelius Christopher Sullivan, but all his friends called him Con. No one knew for sure how old he was. His birth certificate had disappeared years ago. The best guess was somewhere in his late nineties. Grandpa was always smartly dressed in a three-piece suit with a hat and a watch on a chain—except of course, when he was working in the garden.

Luc thought that visiting Grandpa daily wasn't a chore like visiting other relatives. Luc looked forward to their visit each day. Grandpa was always waiting for him as well. Luc could hang with him for hours listening to stories of the fire service in San Francisco, history-making events, and the people that protected this great city. Grandpa's pride in the men he worked with was always present in his tone. Luc always seemed to learn something by the time he went home. Grandpa was pretty cool, he thought. He always seemed to know what was going on with Luc, too, as if he were all-knowing: Even though Luc would not tell him everything about his day, he already knew. It was kinda spooky. Still, Luc thought he was the wisest man in the world.

"Come on, Luc, let's go upstairs and get you a soda. I'm sure you're thirsty after your tryouts. I too have something to discuss. We can help each other."

What did Grandpa mean by that? Luc thought. *No one had snitched on him about sneaking away from the house, had they?* He started to feel wary on the climb up the long stairway to the main entrance of the house.

"Don't you get tired haulin' up and down these stairs, Grandpa?"

"Some days are easier than others. You just got to keep moving at my age, keeps the blood pumping. Strong legs, strong back, strong heart, strong mind." Just then, the dogs came barreling up alongside Luc, knocking him off the stairway and onto a potted plant. Graceful they were not.

Grandpa laughed out loud. "Okay, boys, you can have a treat as well."

Grandpa's house was a landmark formerly used by the fire rescue service back in the day. The grand entry of the parlor always had a constant glow emanating from the large hearth.

"How do you keep that glow in the fireplace so steady?"

Grandpa grinned. "Come in the kitchen, Luc, we can talk there."

The kitchen was large, what one would expect to find in an old firehouse kitchen, with a big stove and wood-burning oven. There was an extended table made of thick mahogany, big pans atop the stove and hanging above the range, and a large frig. Everything was vintage, but all of it was in perfect working condition.

Luc sat at the table as Grandpa pulled a glass beer mug from the freezer with frost on the outside and pried open a cola. He preferred the old glass bottles to the cans or plastic liter bottles, saying the fizz was better.

"There you go, lad. I bet you could you use a cool libation after all that activity." Grandpa turned away to throw the pop cap in the trash.

There he goes again, what does he mean by that? Luc looked at the dogs, and they both turned away, as if to say, "We can't help you now. You're on your own, dude."

Traitors, Luc wanted to say under his breath. Was he getting paranoid about the dogs now, too? He realized he had better fess up before he exploded in remorse. "Grandpa, can we talk?"

"Always, Luc. What do you want to talk about? Anything specific?"

"Something happened today, and I'm not sure how to handle it."

"What is it?"

"Well, I didn't keep my word to Mom. I wandered away from the area today with my friends without asking permission. I knew when I did it it felt wrong. I let my friends pull me along, and I know that's no excuse, either. What do I do?"

"Luc, you don't need me to answer that for you."

Luc lowered his head and regarded the mug of soda, muttering, "I know."

"Sorry, lad. When you're in a storm, taking her head on will always lead you out of harm's way—eventually. Look at the time, your mom will be waiting for you. Time to head home. I think you know what course to set from here. Oh, and here's a thin dime for you." He slipped a folded-up dollar bill into Luc's hand.

"No, Grandpa, no, I don't need anything."

"I know, son, but it makes me feel good." As Luc headed for the door, Grandpa said quietly, "Lots of challenges ahead. Hold your course." Luc looked back from the door. "Maybe you can use it for bus fare when you make that football team this week." Luc almost fell down the stairs. The dogs started barking as if to say, "We told you you can't keep anything from him. He may be old but he isn't stupid!"

Luc's shoulders slumped as he headed down the stairs to face the wrath of a mother wronged.

Chapter Five

LUC RAN WITH EXTENDED STRIDES ALONG THE sidewalk, using the width of each concrete slab as his gauge for every step. As the bark of the dogs faded, his legs grew heavy. With his shoelaces flailing free and his breath catching up to his frantic pace, his sense of victory at making the first cut at football gave way to full-blown apprehension.

Luc's mind was racing. *I could say the phone battery died. Nope, charge still good. Or I could say I had to help Grandpa? Nope, boldfaced lies will get me grounded for sure. Okay, I'm just gonna hit this head on and let the chips fall where they may... listen to Grandpa, don't get too cute. I screwed up, and if I'm locked in my room for the rest of the summer, I deserve it. Well, no I don't, but it could happen. You never know with Mom.*

Luc opened the front door as quietly as he could. But it did not matter. She had those famous mom-ears, the ones mothers got after they had babies and could hear them breathing in their cribs five rooms away with no room monitor on. He ambled casually into the kitchen.

Mom had some sliced carrots waiting for him and a glass of water on the kitchen table. Luc reached for the cookies nearby, snagging two before Mom could bust him.

Now with one hand waving a lone carrot to show he was making a healthful choice, too, his cheeks loaded with cookies, Luc turned away to complete the misdirection play.

"Mom, look, see? Got the carrot." Not his best attempt at misdirection as crumbs flew out of his face while he talked with his mouth full.

His mom looked at him over her shoulder, a look of repulsion and disapproval on her face as she pointedly looked at the now-crumby floor and back up to Luc's face.

"I saw Jack's mom today," she said casually. "What a pleasant talk we had. Haven't seen her for... I don't know how long? You and Jack were hanging out today, right? She was saying how excited Jack was because of summer and that football tryouts were today, or something like that. Did you run into the guys as well?"

"Yeah...?"

"Weren't you cold? It's so foggy and wet outside."

"No... we were cool." *Where is this going?* Luc thought. *Is she baiting me before she slaps me upside the head with her dishtowel?*

"You were cold?"

"No, we were *cool,* Mom."

"Okay, whatever, you and your cool. One day it's *cool* next day it's *sick.* Who can keep up? By the way, you want to tell me about your progress on the back fence?"

"Uh, well, I'm still sanding..."

She turned to raise an eyebrow at him.

"Look, I told Mrs. Martin I would fix everything pretty fast." The words tumbled out of Luc's mouth faster than he could control them. He was babbling now. *Misdirection, don't forget misdirection,* he told himself. "Besides, even if we made a mess, the rescue drill *was* a success."

"Luc, you broke the fence. You ruined the new hedge. Jack's rear end was full of thorns, and you, my little rescue hero, wound up practically on poor Mrs. Martin's lap while she was in the privy. Listen up, Probie, the embarrassment of landing in her lap will be hard to fix."

"But I got out of there superfast. I didn't see anything! And Dad told me that if I had held that Telford line..." A look from his mother indicated that this line of reasoning would only land him in more hot water. Luc's face contorted a bit. "Practice makes perfect?"

Now the dishcloth came flying. "Luuuc!"

"Mom, I'm truly sorry. I promise I won't sit on Mrs. Martin's lap again." Humor was good misdirection, right? Get her in a laughing mood and she'll be less likely to confine you to your room for the rest of your young, innocent life.

"Luc, your antics with this rescue stuff... I mean, I think it's great that you're interested, and your energy and focus are admirable. And I know Con's stories don't help much here. But next time before you jump into something... complicated, shall we say... why don't you read the whole chapter first? We don't need any more injuries. You got it?"

"Yes, ma'am."

"Get your hands washed. Dinner in ten."

Just as Luc was seriously rethinking the timing of his confession, his father shouldered up next to him.

"Wow, never seen you scrub so hard. How about some soap for the old man?"

"What are you doing home?"

"Don't look so surprised! I do live here." Luc's dad was a captain at the fire station at the top of San Francisco's Nob Hill. Following in Grandpa's shoes, Luc's dad had developed a reputation for his leadership of the firefighting team and the rescue skills he taught his team. Only real difference between Grandpa's day as a firefighter and his dad's—besides the equipment and some of the more technical of the maneuvers employed—was that part of Dad's firefighting team now included female firefighters.

Luc continued to scrub his hands alongside his father, tension growing with each slip of his hands against each other.

Great, now I have to tell both of them together. In the past, when Dad was at work, telling Mom sometimes made things easier. By the time it got to Dad, it had been watered down, and they were both usually really cool about things. Mom's version of the story somehow always eased the pain of it reaching Dad's ears. Luc felt sick to his stomach.

"Mom, what's for dinner?"

"We have a nice pasta with red sauce and sausage."

"Cool, I love that stuff, good energy food. Mom, you're the best cook. Garlic bread too, cool. Fight any fires today, Dad?"

"No, son. Just a few car wrecks, jaws of life, that sort of—"

Luc cut in. "No babies to save? No three-story rescue maneuvers to implement? No—"

Luc's dad cut him off. "What's up, Luc?"

"You want to tell us what you want?" His mom was the direct one.

"I don't want anything. And Mom already gave me my marching orders for the back fence."

Luc's dad stifled a laugh while his mom slapped Dad on the back of the head.

Was this the time to hang himself? *One more bite, maybe two. Another piece of garlic bread. Can't talk with the mouth full.*

"Slow down, big guy, you're going to choke. No one's taking it from you."

Hmmmm, choking could help my cause. Instead, he finished chewing and cleared his throat. "Well, there's something I want to talk to you about."

"What's that?'

"Um... football?"

"Is that a question?"

"No, sir."

"Go on."

Luc took a deep breath and then just let it go. "A really great... opportunity came up today, so... I jumped on it..."

"And?" Mom was tightening the noose.

"Well, I always hear you guys say not to let a good opportunity pass you by and..."

"Oh, this is getting good." Dad put down his fork, sat back in his chair, wiped his mouth with the napkin, crossed his arms behind his head, and cocked his head, posturing in anticipation of Luc's next words.

Luc, eyes closed, shoulders pulled up around his ears, said all in one breath, "I kinda... okay, I screwed up today. I... didn't think and went and tried out for football with the guys..."

Luc paused. He did not dare look up at his mom.

"I-I know I did it without permission, but there was no time to ask. I... just did it." Luc finally exhaled and opened one eye to gauge the response. There was a pause. The pause grew longer. He lifted his eyes to see his parents exchanging a long glance. His mother looked less than pleased. But he could not read his dad's expression.

Then his dad blew him away. "Wow! Football! Luc, that sounds great!" His mom looked like she was still absorbing the confession until she heard this and whipped her head to the side to stare at her husband as if he were a madman.

"Was it a tryout?" Dad asked.

Luc exhaled. Maybe his dad was not so peeved? "Yeah, and I made the first cut. So did the guys."

"Really? That's exciting. You know your old man here played a little ball in his day. Wasn't half bad, either." Joe Sullivan was proud of his athletic prowess, constantly showing off his muscles for his wife, Dorothy.

Mrs. Sullivan just rolled her eyes and shook her head. Luc darted his eyes away the second she glared at him. "Okay, Green Bay Packers Aaron Rodgers," Mom said, glaring at his dad. "Now back to the real question." She gave Captain Sullivan the fish eye. "Let's talk about what screw-up, Luc. I mean the *real* screw-up? Not the football tryouts."

"I didn't make quarterback?" Humor to deflect?

"Luc!" Nope. She was not buying it.

At this point Luc could see the water begin to bubble inside his mom's head. Next would come the spits of steam from the ears. The silence was deafening, four adult eyes focused intently on Luc.

With lips tight she faked a wide smile, her eyes piercing through him. Luc's mom, in her own frustrated way, was just waiting for a straight answer.

Luc was lily-livered. He said not a word.

"Not happy about this! Not one bit." She was now gracing him with the same stink eye she had bestowed upon his dad.

Luc exhaled a long sigh and crunched in his shoulders. "Mom, I'm sorry, I left the area without permission and took the streetcar up to McCoppin Field for the tryouts. I got lost in all the excitement, and the guys, you know..."

"No I don't know. What if something happened to you? What if you got hurt? You know better!"

Luc knew he had broken her trust. *Okay, now I've done it. Here comes the silent treatment while she figures out five ways to choose from how to make my life miserable. Not good. What do I say? I deserve it. That's the problem. I deserve it.*

Dad interjected. They both knew Mom from their years of experience with her. "Sweetie, hold on a second, can I say something?"

"Go ahead. I'm already getting a headache."

"Luc, all the things your mom is saying are true. But really, this time, no harm no foul. The last thing we want to do is worry your mom. But I can understand, under the circumstances, how things got revved up with the guys."

Luc wanted to hug his dad. What a good guy.

"Now, more importantly, what position do you think you want to play, or where do you think they want you?"

His mom looked at his dad as if to say, "Traitor!" And Luc could tell that even though she was getting a headache, she was also getting her second wind.

"You might not realize this, young man slash world traveler of the Sunset District, but this is a small neighborhood, and we parents can text as well." Mom lowered her voice. "I've got spies everywhere." It started to dawn on Luc. Maybe she was joshing him? No... Then she hit him with it.

"Even though you broke the rules, you didn't keep it from us. It was *ultimately* very responsible of you to realize right from wrong and then try to fix it. Now sit and eat the best meal you're going to get till you turn thirty. By the way, we knew hours ago where you and the boys were. Just wanted to let you stew a while. If you took too much longer I was going to have Dad hang you by your toes. More importantly, I think you're a receiver type... You know, maybe a tight end."

Luc could feel his eyes bulging out of his head like a cartoon character's when he realized he had been had. "What? I didn't know you knew about football!"

"You bet!" Dad said. "Your mom wasn't half bad in her old powder puff league."

"That's enough out of you." She was really honing her talents with the dishtowel as a weapon, Luc noted.

"Yes, sweetie, anything you say," Dad replied, choking back a smile. "So what's your practice schedule?"

"What do you wear?" Mom wanted to know. "And you need to stay hydrated. Drink your milk for strong bones. That tackling can be rough."

"Remember fundamentals," Dad added.

"You know, you guys are pretty cool," Luc said. And he meant it. He had caught a rare break this time.

Mom looked slightly proud of herself. At least she was amused.

Dad was just grinning. "Play hard, have fun, and be a good sport. Football will give you plenty of life lessons."

Mom cut in. "And you *will* find time to finish that broken fence, turn the soil and fertilize the hedge, and fix Mrs. Martin's... whatever she wants. Poor creature. Thirteen-year-old boy comes crashing into her bathroom while she's on the toilet..."

"Surprised she didn't croak right then and there," Dad said, laughing.

"Joe!"

"Yes, ma'am?"

"Don't teach your son to be disrespectful."

Luc's phone began to vibrate. A text. Luc felt for his phone beneath the table and peeked. He was not supposed to use electronics at the table.

"U busted?" It was from Jack.

"No. Lucky."

"Cn I come ovr? Toss a ball?"

"Y."

"K. C u in 20."

Luke lifted his eyes. His parents were staring him down.

"Busted!" they both chorused.

Luc's mom got up and moved toward the sink, muttering. "Does he really think we were born yesterday?"

His dad got up and chuckled, nuzzling the back of her hair as his arms encircled her from behind. "Weren't our parents clueless when we were his age?"

"Hmmph!"

Luc took the opportunity of their gross show of affection to slip his plate and glass into the sink and make a beeline for his room. While he did not want to push his luck today, he did want to practice throwing the ball with his best bud. Best to get out of their sight, and maybe out of their minds.

Chapter Six

THE NEXT DAY GRANDPA WATCHED FROM THE FRONT step as Luc and the dogs played a mean game of fetch the slobbery tennis ball. By the time Luc was played out, the ball was so shredded and sopping with drool he was tempted to toss it right in the trash. Just as he attempted a Michael Jordan lob, Grandpa stood up.

"Time to get serious, kid."

Luc held the ball out as a tease to get the dogs lumbering up the stairs and into the house. He washed his hands and sat as Grandpa made them both a cup of hot cocoa. Then, warmed by the cozy fire, Luc settled in for another story.

"In New York City a conflagration so large hit Manhattan that it became known as the Great Wall Street Fire. The year was 1835, and the fire began in a five-story warehouse at 25 Merchant Street in the Wall Street area. It was chilly as all get out, and the winds were blowing so fiercely the temperature had dropped to 17 degrees Fahrenheit. It was so cold that fire responders had to cut ice from the East River to get water. Then the water froze in the hoses and pumps. The fire was spreading fast with the gale force winds, eating up hundreds and hundreds of buildings, some of them new stores with iron gratings that prevented the firefighters from getting in—not that it would have made much difference. Fighting fire with chunks of ice is a losing endeavor."

"Big bummer!" said Luc.

"Indeed," agreed Grandpa.

"Two people were killed. The damage was estimated at twenty million dollars, which today would be hundreds of millions of dollars. It was a total disaster."

The fire in the hearth began smoking more than usual as sparks popped out of the wood. Grandpa looked up from his knot tying. At that moment, Luc was again trying on the battle-worn fire helmet from the mantle.

"Luc, put that back! It's not time!"

But it was too late. Out of the corner of his eye, Luc noticed Grandma's concertina on the chair, then... Crash! Bang! Plop! In an instant Luc found himself disheveled and sitting on the cobblestone curb outside the Rose Street fire hall in New York City. All the buildings and streets looked different: old, dusty, blackened by coal and dirt. And it was freezing cold. The big fire hall in front of him, Knickerbocker Number 12, told him the name of the fire company.

Luc overheard a Marine in full dress. "I heard they called us in case we got to blow up the buildings in the path of the beast. Won't make no difference if she eats up block after block with this evil wind."

It had been a tough night so far for these men, the first round of volunteers fighting the fire, and the smell of dense smoke had a commanding presence. It was everywhere and on everything. Was the battle even close to being won? Luc had no idea.

"Hey, kid, get out there and get some wood and coal for the stove. We're freezing!" someone yelled.

Luc cranked his head. *Are they talking to me?* Exhausted and frozen, the firefighters did not seem to notice that Luc was oddly clothed and looked out of place. He guessed they assumed he was just a young recruit or runner.

Luc realized they were looking directly at him with quizzical expressions in their eyes. "Yes, sir! Right away, sir!" He shouted out to be heard above the noise and bustle as a new wave of firefighters passed into Knickerbocker 12. "Um, where exactly is it?" Luc asked sheepishly.

A large man stepped forward. "For Pete's sake, go see William, William Tweed. He'll show you how to run. Over there!"

The man pointed. Luc turned to see the boy—for he appeared not much older than Luc—they called William, whose arms were loaded with anything that would burn, setting it down next to a nearby potbellied stove.

Luc rushed over. "I'm here to help. I'm Luc Sullivan."

Will, with a hurried nod at Luc, said, "Good, good to meet yah. Will, Will Tweed is my name."

For some reason Luc thought the boy looked familiar. William might have been near or past 13 years old, but he already looked like a hardened, street-savvy runner. The runners were the ones who did the bidding of the firefighters, helping to keep the station running, fetching coal and wood, keeping Knickerbocker 12 and other stations clean—even cooking for the men if they were close to the age of being recruited. All runners had one goal: to grow into the shoes of their heroes, the firefighters of Knickerbocker 12 and other fire halls across the cities and towns of every state in the country.

"Okay, start breakin' this here up to size for the old potbelly. Over there." Will indicated with his chin. "The way she's been eatin' up that building from what I hear, seems like she's hungrier than any of the other fires I seen so far—though I pray she's not hungry forever."

Your mouth to the ears of heaven, Luc thought. Luc did as he was told. The boys worked efficiently side by side, getting the oven fired up and even putting up some water for coffee and tea for the men who came in from the cold, breathing frosty air out of their mouths as they huddled near the stove, rubbing their hands together to shake off the cold.

A firefighter came up to William and patted his back. "Don't know what we would do without you runner volunteers here to keep us comfortable," said a grizzled man, filthy with black from head to toe.

Luc watched as Will blushed fiercely.

"You're respected here among the men, Will Tweed. You'll make a fine recruit in a few years."

"Yes, sir," Will replied humbly.

Luc smiled. He knew how good it felt when seasoned firefighters appreciated the efforts put forth by wannabes like Will—and like him for that matter. He went outside again to fetch more wood and came back in trembling so hard he dropped a few pieces from his overloaded arms.

"Whoa, Nellie!" said Will, reaching forward to help Will unload. "You done this before?"

"Yeah. I volunteer after school at my dad's fire hall. He's a captain."

"You go to school still? I'm a workin' since I was a wee lad."

Luc wondered where he was that a kid did not have to go to school by law.

"Where you come from? Not from around here, I can see that," Will said, appraising Luc and his twenty-first-century clothing.

Luc did not know what to say about that. But he was quickly getting so filthy he would soon blend right in with the other runners and volunteers who seemed to be growing in number as the minutes passed. The fire was probably getting worse. Luc hoped his height would set him apart, make him seem older and more capable then the other boys milling about outside the hall, waiting to be called upon to do something important.

Luc glanced around. The equipment was not in the house to look over, but he thought he saw big clumps of hay and horse manure on the floor in the big hall. "Uh, Will, what day is this?"

"Who cares?" Will grunted. "If we don't keep helping them all recoup, the volunteers cannot be ready for the next fire." Luc picked up a twinge of an Irish accent.

As Luc was sizing wood for the stove, he picked up a newspaper. *New York Evening Post. Published semi-weekly for the city and its citizens. December 16, 1835.*

"What?" Luc nearly fell down on his butt right there in the fire hall kitchen. Grandpa had just been telling him about the Great Fire of 1835. Was this where he was? And was this the Great Wall Street Fire? Was he dreaming? He socked himself in the arm. Nope. That really hurt. This was real. *The squeezebox—that's what did it. That's how I got here. It's not just the helmet. It's a combination of the two. It's like a fire starter kit: put on the helmet and grab my grandmother's old squeezebox and off I fly into another time, another place.* He had done this before, but he had no idea how he was going to get back again. And this time he was afraid. More at stake here if it really was 1835. Did they even suspect what they were in for?

Luc got back to work in a daze. Will, working feverishly, paused and looked at him impatiently.

"No need to read the paper. We got a lot to do. I hear the fire's a hungry monster. Don't care nothin' for them who's tryin' to stop her. Lucky she's confined so far to one building, from what I been hearin' from the boys."

They both continued to work, but Luc was putting two and two together, realizing how catastrophic this fire was to going be and knowing he could do nothing to halt its course. He knew the Marine Corps would sometime soon gather gunpowder from the Brooklyn Navy Yard to blow up more buildings in the fire's wake, but he could not exactly tell Will that. Nor could he tell Will that the effort to fight this fire would prove largely fruitless.

"Has anyone died yet?" Luc asked softly.

"What did you say?" Will asked. "No one's dead."

Luc nodded. *I almost gave it* away, he thought. He also thought that Will felt somehow strangely familiar to him. Luc did not know why, but he already felt like Will was similar to the guys back home.

Luc glanced at another sheet of the newspaper as he was feeding it into the hearth. He watched it, mesmerized as he remembered how he had gotten here what seemed like only moments ago.

"Come on, Sully, time to work."

How did he know my nickname?

As if reading his mind, the other boy said, "We got a Sullivan here. Goes by Sully. Assume you all do, right? Well, any old way, we be needin' to get 'hold of a new king bolt for Old Knickerbocker Number 12. Snapped like a twig during the fire and put that rig out o' service for a time. The bandage we used ain't goin' to last."

Luc already knew the fire was soon going to engulf much of Wall Street. While there were bells at each firehouse, there was no proper revolving alert system in place. Masonry buildings of five to seven stories were out of reach of the largest ladders available to the volunteers. And these buildings, a lot of them recently upgraded with copper roofing and refitted in an overhaul of the neighborhood, were valuable property, as they housed an agglomeration of businesses that served the economic life of not only New York but also the nation.

To the north of Knickerbocker 12 was the residential district. The only gauntlet in the path to slow the onslaught of flames in that direction was rows of merchants, banks, exchanges, and business buildings of all types, including the huge coffee house known to all as the Tontine Building. The buildings stood side by side, like soldiers at attention. But they had nowhere to go, and nothing could stop a powerful fire if she decided to grow. Could Luc tell Will where the fire would travel? Would Will even believe him? Would Luc alter history if he offered up this information? Grandpa never said what to do or gave any instructions about what was expected of him in his time travels, only making vague comments about historical factoids that were interesting and all, but left Luc feeling somewhat frustrated. "You got to think for yourself, son," Luc remembered his dad saying just the other day when Luc stood before the pile of wood fencing that he was supposed to prep for building. So many riddles.

"You'll know what to do, Luc, you'll know when something happens how to handle it," was all Grandpa would say. "You'll be fine, trust your instincts." But Grandpa had known where he was going every trip he had taken before; in those other time travel experiences, Luc was supposed to be just a spectator. Now he had a mission to find Florian's amulet. He looked around him. And where would he start to look for that?

He shivered, smelling the smoke as a gust of frigid wind blew into the room when someone opened the fire hall front doors to haul in some haggard-looking horses untethered from any equipment.

"I'm a little scared," Luc wanted to say. But he was afraid the other boy would scoff. Will Tweed looked tough, ready for anything.

"Remember the greater good, lad." Luc heard the echo of his grandfather's words.

Will interrupted Luc's thoughts. "Sully, you're one strange kid, always talkin' to yer self. But I'm mighty grateful you're a good worker."

Just after 9:00 P.M., Will and Sully left the firehouse, warm and stocked with coal and wood, and went on the prowl, not being able to resist their boyish curiosity about the tragedy unfolding before their eyes. They were in shouting distance of the business district known as lower Manhattan.

Will, now wearing a thick jacket taken from a hook in the firehouse, still pocketed his hands and had to bend forward to fight the wind.

They heard a commotion up ahead. Luc saw a leather-head, a city watchman wearing a helmet just like the one at Grandpa's. "That leatherhead's name is Thomas Hayes. He patrols the city every night. Ever'body down here knows'm," Will commented. He was much more comfortable around Luc now, their shared experience working side by side for hours binding them closer, faster than would happen under other circumstances. But in an emergency, everything moved faster, Luc noted.

"Officer Hayes!" called Will. "Over here, it's me, Will Tweed."

"Ah, young Will!" The older man was out of breath. "'Tis an unmerciful night, this is."

"How'd she start?" Will asked.

"Started over at 25 Merchant Street, a five-story full of dry goods. We closed the doors, but the beast got a lot of headway before we did and the wind whipped 'er up. Looks like a gas pipe broke. You can still hear the whistling as it feeds the fire."

Luc knew from Dad and Grandpa that you needed to shut down the source at the gas main.

"Probably lose all them buildings near it down there if she grows," said Will grimly.

"Need to call out more volunteers," Hayes declared. "Men down there getting beat by the effort to stop 'er.

Not making much headway. She's hungrier than any fire I ever did see." Officer Hayes twirled his wooden stick absently, staring off into the distance, then covering his mouth as he coughed from the smoke. "Best you go back to Knickerbocker 12 and sound them bells again. Night's not nearly over yet."

Will nodded. "We'll go back, but Mr. Hayes, do ye by any chance have a spare king bolt? Knickerbocker 12's snapped in the last fire."

"Back of the wagon, Will," Hayes said. "I got more nuts 'n bolts 'n carpenter's tools then all them back at the firehouse. What with my finishing business and—"

Will interrupted the officer with a gasp that made him inhale so hard that he broke out coughing, and Luc had to pound him on the back to help him get it all out. "Oh no! My mom is workin' late tonight. She be the accountant and bookkeeper for a business at 27 Merchant Street! Oh, Lord. My mom! Don't take my mom. Sully, I need to go! You have to get back to the fire hall and sound the alarm and make sure they know more men is going t' be needed. Make haste, my new friend. New York is depending on you."

"But, Will, your mom... I can help."

"Go! Go now! I'll see you back here where the fight is raging." They both took off in different directions, disappearing into the ever-expanding smoke that had already began to engulf the streets, making it hazy even in the dark of night.

Chapter Seven

AN OMINOUS GLOW BEGAN TO FILL THE NIGHT SKY over Manhattan, and people began to gather. The streets filled with business owners as well as others from all walks of life. The leatherheads were gathering to ward off looters, a problem that would build like a fire, often impossible to stop. Luc made his way back to the fire hall, ready to give the company details. Volunteers stood ready to go. They could see the great bright light in the sky from blocks away.

"Kid, you got the king bolt?" a rescue officer asked.

"Yes, sir, hope this is the one," Luc said breathlessly. "Will Tweed said it was."

"What do ya got for us on the fire?"

Luc's excitement and nerves were getting the better of him. He could hardly put a sentence together. "Leatherheads... 25 Merchant Street, totally involved. Will's mom... wind spreading, gas, imminent collapse... brick..."

"Calm down son, you've done well, I got it. We'll be out of here as soon as we finish the repair. Now turn around and get back there, and get some more boys to light the way for us with these torches."

In 1835, Luc knew, responding to a fire at night was dangerous and difficult. A one-ton rig with the engine rolling was hard to stop with only men to push and pull it, and injuries were common. Hydrants were difficult to locate in the dark, and they were sometimes hidden from sight with barrels. Volunteers came from all directions to fight the fire, and there was a competition to be the first to get water *on* the fire.

"First water gets the insurance money, boys." The foreman would shout. Sometimes a fight between companies would preempt any sort of firefighting and rescue at all. Luc was intent on getting back to help Will and his mom, while also finishing his tasks to assist the volunteers. His work included lighting the way for Knickerbocker Number 12 and locating hydrants, then concealing them by putting a barrel over them. Knickerbocker Number 12 would have the hydrant first.

As he rounded the corner of the 25 Merchant Street address, the radiant heat from the building, now totally involved, kept him at bay. The smoke was thick and pressurized as it spewed from the roof. It gushed out of all the floors and windows like lava flowing from a volcano. Flames were now present in all the windows, scuttles, and stairwells. Nothing could possibly survive this inferno. Safe distances had to be maintained, because a collapse was imminent. Brick was not as fireproof as people thought. Exposure buildings were the ones threatened now, and they became the focus of the volunteers. Luc got to 25 Merchant Street, but not without absorbing superheated gases from the structure. Unstoppable flying embers transferred heated gases from building to building as Luc could see the roofs of the buildings behind the warehouse now looking like they were catching fire. And 27 Merchant Street was next in line, smoke already puffing through the eaves. This could only mean one thing: fire was in the walls and already running the attic.

All of sudden an alarm rang out from Luc's smartphone. It was losing its charge and in the red. It pulled his focus from the fire. But he remembered what Grandpa had said about thinking on his feet and trusting his instincts. Luc now realized the alarm was the trigger to return to the present. Time was tightning at both ends. He needed to help Will, but he also needed to get back.

How was he even supposed to prepare for his return trip to the present? He had never worried about that before, as it had just happened. The window was closing on the conveyor home, and if he missed it, all would be lost in the fight to save Will and his mother. For Luc, it didn't make sense. *If I leave I can't help, if I stay I can't help.* But he was certain of one thing. Grandpa knew best.

The sense of urgency was now at a critical stage. Rescue was always the first goal of any fire strategy and tactical maneuver. Luc surveyed the situation and made entry into 27 Merchant Street only to find his new friend, Will Tweed, sitting at the foot of the open stairwell. Will was unable to make his way up to his mother on the fifth floor because of the debilitating smoke engulfing the area. Will looked lost and defeated. Then he saw Luc. "You came back."

"Never leave a friend. Two in two out."

Will looked surprised. Such loyalty from someone he barely knew must seem unusual. But he was now focused on saving his mother. "Luc, my mom, she's all I got. I can't even get up the stairs!"

"We need to get out of here now, or we will lose to this fire."

"I will not be leavin' my mother. Have you lost your mind?"

Luc grabbed Will at the shoulders and squared up to him. "Will, you have to trust me. I have an idea, and it's our only shot. Now let's go!"

Luc watched Will realize in an instant that he had few options. Fire was licking up against them from within the walls surrounding them. Will reluctantly began to leave as he listened intently to what Luc was saying.

"All right, here's the plan." As Luc spoke, he thought about what Grandpa would do. "We need to go to the next building." Luc turned and set off running.

"Where you going? That building is not on fire!" Will shouted after him.

Luc knew that to get to Will's mother, he had only one option: the exposure building next door. He needed to use it to get on the fire building, roof to roof.

"Will, we're going to get your mother out. We need a ladder—a roofing ladder—you know with large hooks on the ends of the beams. And I need two hundred-foot ropes as well. Get them from the trucks that are staging. Get them now!"

"Righty!" said Will, clearly relieved to do something, anything to help. "An' the chief, Gullick, be here now. He will get this under control if anyone can."

Luc turned to see that a large man, tall and strong and in full firefighting gear, had arrived and taken command. With the chief out in front, any squabbles over whose fire it was had been laid to rest. If not, Chief Gullick was known to deal with such lack of focus with an iron fist, figuratively and literally. Every man knew: to be walloped by the chief was like getting kicked in the head by a mule.

"Chief! I'm Luc Sullivan, working with Will Tweed as a runner."

"Out of my way, son. We've got a fire to fight, and we're chasing it right now."

"You don't understand. Will's mother is in that building, 27 Merchant, and trapped."

"Can't spare a soul right now, boy. What we've got going on here will make a difference and save his mother, I hope."

Luc was now thinking about ventilation as he spied a spare pumper at the corner. He saw a group of runners and leatherheads, all likely future volunteers, standing by for orders. He ran to them and said, "Will Tweed's mother is trapped on one of the upper floors of 27. Will needs all of you."

"We have no water, and no hydrants! They're all froze up," shouted one in the group.

"We need to pump fresh air into the building, push out and ventilate the smoke."

They all looked at him curiously, wondering who this boy was. But in the heat of the moment, it did not make a difference. Luc had given them information with great authority. They began to position the apparatus and connect the hoses.

"Luc, what be happenin'?" Will had returned. "Here's the ladder and rope you asked for."

"The boys will be pumping fresh air into the area where your mother's located to keep her from being overcome by the smoke. I'll explain later, but it's PPV, 'positive pressure ventilation.' Trust me, it's really cool."

Will shot him a look. "Cool?"

"Expedites the rescue," Luc said.

Will frowned.

"Never mind! It'll work!"

Miraculously listening to this kid from wherever, everyone began to ferry the large ladder up the side of the building vertically, floor by floor. It was impossible for such a large ladder to make its way up the interior of the stairwell of the 29 street address, so they worked from outside. Luc had secured the bitter end of the rope to the last rung of the ladder with a knot his grandpa had taught him: the bowline, one of the better all-around knots.

As the two boys worked together running floor to floor to assist each other in relaying the ladder upward, the fire roared on unabated in 25 Merchant Street, quickly auto-exposing and spreading to 27 next door. The boys reached the roof and maneuvered the ladder over the parapet wall.

"Now what, Sully?" Will asked.

"Let me take a quick look at what we got. We need to check all sides." Luc got to the side of the building to be bridged and stopped in his tracks.

"Oh, no."

"What is it, what's wrong?" Will shouted, running to Luc's side.

"Oh no is right." Will saw then what Luc saw: His mother's building was not as tall as the one they were on. "Now what?"

Luc started thinking about what Grandpa or Dad would do. "Will, I got it!"

"What?"

"We need to get the ladder below to the next floor that's level with the other roof, then bridge it, okay? We'll lower it down, hook the edge to the roof, and we'll come down, and then bridge from the window. Got it? Simple!"

"Are you mad?" Will exclaimed.

"No, not at all... I saw it in Grandpa's old rope manual. If it's in there, it must work. Anyway, the ladder is too big to get down interior stairs. Let's go, we're wasting time! Will, you go to the floor below, and I'll lower the ladder to you below the windowsill so you can pull the hooks in first, so when we bridge, the foot will land first, on the other side."

"Have you ever done this before?"

"Well, not exactly, but I've read all about it. That's all I need."

Will shook his head. Somehow this kid from out of nowhere was navigating all these obstacles.

Everything went smoothly, considering neither one had ever done anything like this before. Luc held the rope as best he could while Will struggled to get the ladder up and in. At the same time, Luc's hands began to chafe and bleed from the rope. Luc got below with Will and started rigging.

"After we bridge the building, we'll get to your mom from the interior light well. During the size-up, I saw that the tradesman's entrance to 27 Merchant Street led to the basement and light well. Time's a wasting, let's go."

"That's cool!" Will stopped in his tracks. "Whatever that means."

Luc could tell Will's confidence was back, and he was ready to do anything for his mother. Will straddled the roofing ladder and watched intently as Luc configured the rope four to five rungs from the foot.

"Shouldn't we tie this from the top?" Will asked.

"The reason we tie from the foot on this side is to be able to lower the foot onto the building first from this side. Since we'll be working in tight quarters on the fire building, we'll be able to directly feed the ladder into the light well without having to flip it over. Then the roofing hooks will fit nicely onto the lip of the light well."

All the while, the fire building was burning with ever mounting and overwhelming heat, smoke, and flame. They could actually see and feel the pressure expanding in the walls of the brick edifice. Gasping for air and choking, the two boys continued their mission unfazed, always aware of their surroundings. Luc and Will kept moving forward, refusing to give up.

"We're gonna get Mom, right Sully?"

Luc was sucking wisps of air from the rooftop floor and coughing. "Will," Luc said with a determined look, "better start planning what you and your mom will be doing for Christmas dinner. Hear she's a good cook."

"How'd you hear th—" Will stopped short as he realized Luc was just trying to get his mind off the immediate danger and into the realm of success.

Luc reached for the rope and measured two fathoms, then began to work the bitter end over the seventh measured rung and around the beam. He pulled parallel across to the opposite beam and rung. He brought enough through to attach with an equalizing bowline. Both sides were identical.

"Sully, where did you learn that?"

"Grandpa has me practice this one all the time. Now help me get this to vertical on the windowsill, on the edge of the building. Watch your step. The first one is a doozy. Here, now you foot the ladder." As soon as they stood up in the window they could feel the radiant heat sweep across the roof of the building they were about to bridge.

"Let's hope we have enough throw on this ladder." Instead of hand over hand, Luc let the rope slide between his hands, unaware that tearing skin from his hands was worse than the pain or blistering of radiant heat. That would be the price of lowering the ladder without gloves.

"Will, you're letting it slide. Put your weight into it." They missed the opposite roof. Now Will had a good foot on it; however, with layers of skin starting to come off, Luc was left to hoist the ladder back up for a second attempt.

"I think I got it this time," Will said. "I'm sorry. I won't let you down again. It just slipped."

"That's all right, let's get your mom." Luc's hands were bleeding and the sting was worse than it looked—and that was pretty bad, he saw, though the light from the fire barely let him see up close.

"Oh, your hands." Will grimaced.

"Don't remind me. We've got to get over to that roof. We don't have much time." With an unstable ladder in place, Luc had Will go first, knowing that he had a good anchor point stabilizing his path.

"Don't look down, Will. Keep moving." With fiery gusts of wind carrying embers above and windows belching fire below, Will could not help but look down. With that, Luc's fear of Will freezing in the middle of the crawl came true.

"Sully! I'm slipping!"

"Will, you're okay. You have to keep moving. You're almost across. Relax and breathe. You'll be fine. Just concentrate on moving forward."

Will regained some faith from Luc's counsel, but he moved forward slowly.

For Luc, the pace made it seem like an eternity. There was still much to be done, not to mention he needed to cross as well with Will holding the other side.

"Will, look! You made it. Now hold on for me."

Luc talked himself across the bridge. "Tell yourself what you just told Will, don't look down, stay focused, move steady." He scrambled like a circus monkey on fire.

"You sure made that look easy," Will remarked.

"Trust me, it was easier to tell you how to do it. I better check my pants. Okay, Will, stay low from the heat. We'll drag the foot of the ladder to the light well. Then I'll tie the ladder again and prepare for lowering into the well. Got it?"

"Got it." All of sudden you could hear Will's mom from the light well. Her voice echoed upward with fear and helplessness. Will reached over the side and said, "Mom, we're here for ya, hold on. We'll save ya!"

"Tell your mom to stay low and in the window so she can get fresh air—and stay away from the heat." Luc could now see the vertical tie he had made originally. He cleaned it up.

"Okay, Will, ready? Now extend the ladder over the side. When it reaches its leverage spot, it should go vertical and slide down the wall. I got the rope. You make sure it's getting down the wall properly."

Will took an occasional peek, shading his face from the heat. The light well was lit up like a flickering Christmas tree. The windows had not yet blown out, but with the glow of the fire within, you could feel the awesome pressure mounting.

"Will, make sure the ladder doesn't break any windows. If it breaks a window and allows oxygen to feed the fire, we would be blown up for sure." As the ladder settled in place, they realized they had come up too short.

"Oh, so not cool." Luc was really stymied now, and nervous to boot. "Good news and bad news. Bad news, we're short. Good news, your mom is within reach of the lower two rungs. Bad news, fire's ready to break into the light well at any moment. More bad news: I've got to go down and secure her with a sling and get her out of the window and on the ladder. And more bad news—"

"Wait, wait, wait." Will said. "Is there any more good news?"

"I'm sorry. I'm just thinking out loud. Let's do this! Will, secure the ladder with rope to the air vent. I'll make a hasty harness out of this webbing I'm carrying. Comes in handy." The second rope was now attached to Luc by way of a bowline on a bite.

"This way, when I get to your mom, I can pick her off quickly." Luc was over the edge and down the ladder. With every step he encountered more heat. All he could focus on was Will's mom. As he reached the final rung, he extended the sling to her.

"Hi, I'm Sully, uh, Luc, Will's friend. Ready to go?" Even amid all that was life threatening, Luc stayed composed enough to instruct the application of the sling to Will's mom. After it was on, Luc loosened his belt just enough to extend the buckle to attach to the sling.

"I love this belt made out of webbing and a cara-biner... who woulda thunk something so simple..." With

Will's mom secured to the belt, Luc yelled up to Will for a pull.

"Slack, Will, haul away slowly." Will's mom reached for the last rung with her left foot, then the right.

"One step at a time, Mrs. Tweed." With that said, one of the windows blew out. The force was not enough to impinge on their ascent, but certainly enough to put a little hitch in their giddyup. As they got their legs over the lip of the light well to safety, what used to be a threatening fire was now an inferno. With a quick glance, Luc eyed a strange green detail in the orange fiery mass licking from within. *Out of place? Yes. Time to analyze? No way.* His only thought, *Let's keep moving.* Now as if chasing him the windows had given in to the heat, and there was auto-exposing up. The light well was now a chimney with fire and gases releasing upward and hot on their tails. As mother and son engaged in a hug, Luc was thinking, *Just in time.*

"Okay, you two, we're now on the fire building, and it's running the attic. We've got to get across the bridge again—now!"

Will and his mom looked at each other. "That's Sully. Knows it all. I admit it's a little strange, but he knows what he's doing."

"I should say so." His mom smiled appreciatively. "Thank you, Sully. Thank you with all my heart."

"I appreciate that, ma'am, but thank me later when we're a bit safer and over there."

Luc reached and secured the bridging tie. "Will, foot it again and lower it onto the other side."

"Hey, Luc! Gettin' the hang of this now."

With the pain of tearing skin from his hands all over Luc's face, they lowered into place. "Okay, Will, show your mom how it's done. Second time's easier, right?"

Will, feeling that they were almost home free, got to the other side. With Luc and Will on either side stabilizing the ladder, Mom scurried across and into the window.

"Way to go, Mom!" Luc yelled. It had been a harrowing experience for this woman. He felt as warm inside as the air felt around him.

The fire and smoke were now at a point where they had engulfed the entire roof.

"Luc, hurry, hurry!" they urged him. Luc made it onto the parapet wall with Will stabilizing the ladder for his return. The smoke was now so dense no one could see. Luc looked down as his smartphone alarm went off. The ladder shook uncontrollably as the fire extended through 27 Merchant, and the brick began to give way below. Collapse was coming. The brick façade was crumbling. Because of the smoke, Will could not see, but only felt the sudden release. The foot of the ladder from the other side had slipped off the edge and was dragging his side along. It fell and with it... Luc tumbled between the buildings.

"Sullyyyyyyy! Noooooo!" Will cried out. "I didn't let go, I had you, I put my weight into it like you taught me! Noooooo!" Will turned to his mother in disbelief, his head in his hands. "Mom... me friend!"

"I know, son, I know." Will had only known Sully for a few hours, but what they experienced together was like living a lifetime. Will Tweed would never forget Luc Sullivan.

The speed of the descent had returned Luc to the conveyor as he began his helpless tumble home. Crash! Bang! Plop! Luc was back through the fireplace portal and in the present. Luc looked at his hands. They were unscathed. He looked up to see his grandpa.

"Grandpa, is there something you wanted to say before I left?"

Grandpa gave a little chuckle. "Your friend Will and his mom are safe. You saved them. So let me get you something to eat first. Then you have homework. The rest can wait till tomorrow."

Chapter Eight

THE FOLLOWING AFTERNOON, LUC AND THE DOGS bounded in on Grandpa in the living room. Grandpa was holding one of his many journals. He shifted his reading glasses down his nose, peering over them. "You know, Will and his mom consider you a hero."

Luc was overwhelmed. "I wanted to do the right thing. I just didn't know if I was doing everything right."

"Better to do something rather than nothing. Lives usually depend on it.

"Grandpa, I saw an odd green spot or something in the fire, I was think..."

"Luc, I told you this story had to be told in bits and pieces in order for you to understand. If you're willing to continue, and you're patient with me, we'll continue our journey."

"Okay, let's do it."

"You have now experienced what you were meant to do—your calling. In essence, you now embody what a firefighter does. Yet this journey manifests itself in a way that calls for your trust and faith."

Luc's head was spinning. "So what I experienced wasn't a dream? Then I was really there?" The full realization of what happened set in. He marveled, "I actually saved Will and his mother in 1835?"

"Yes, Luc. With today's adventure and the others to come, you will learn more about your fate. You were there, fulfilling your mission of saving lives and preserving history."

"You gotta be kiddin' me. Wait till my friends hear about this! Do Mom and Dad know? When do I go again? Will I miss football practice? Will I be back in time for dinner?"

"Hold your horses, lad. Let's not be hasty about this." Grandpa looked pleased but cautious. "You must keep this secret to yourself. No one can know."

"Am I time traveling?"

"Yes, and it's true. The event has already occurred in history. Your mission is a rescue adventure. You will be interacting with great names of the past, as well as everyday folk. Nonetheless, every one of them will be important to history and the families and firefighters involved in that historical event."

Luc picked up a journal. "This journal says 1906."

"April to be exact, Luc. This journal belonged to Chemical Company Number 5, located at 410 Bush Street in San Francisco."

"The San Francisco earthquake and fire! This journal isn't in as good a shape as your others on the shelf."

"Suffice to say, that book did better than most that day." Grandpa said.

"Is this my next trip?"

"Could be. However, all conditions must be... right."

"What? Why? Can't I just go?"

"Luc, remember what happened when you were holding the leather helmet?"

"Yeah, I ended up in New York... Ohhhhh! If I touch the helmet I'm gone."

"Not quite. You could wear that helmet all day long and nothing would happen. You need a couple of other elements. You see Grandma's squeezebox?"

"Yeah. You mentioned that before. I need that too? I thought maybe that had something to do with all this."

"You know the fire in the hearth you always ask about?"

"Yeah, the Greek fire."

"Well, it's not for me to say when you travel, but the combination of those three elements and your commitment to rescue, as well as the preservation of history, are all part of this mix. You will learn that in your exploits, your work will counter any dark influences that could change history. What you think should be done at times might not be the best outcome for history in the future—that, my boy, will be the greatest challenge in these journeys, and in your life: trying to balance your own needs with the greater good. Sometimes you'll have to take a step back and make a quick decision. For if history is changed, destiny and the future as we know it will be gone forever.

"How can you change history?"

"It's a difficult concept. Imagine all of time happening at once... past, present, and future."

"That's hard to wrap my brain around."

"I know, son. Let me ask you, Luc, how did your friend Will do at football today?"

"What does Will have to do with... ? Wait a minute... Will? Is my new friend Will from New York the same..."

"Yes and no. Will Tweed's mom is your friend Will's great-great-great grandmother. He was named after her husband."

"No way! That is so cool!"

Luc was pumped. "Grandpa, let's do this thing. I can help. I promise I'll make good decisions." Then he paused for a moment. "But can I still play football?"

"Pay attention, Luc. Time is of the essence, both the past and future." Grandpa settled back into his favorite leather chair. "Now let me tell you about that day in 1906. It was a Wednesday, the 18th of April at 5:12 A.M., right here in San Francisco. Most everyone was asleep.

"Suddenly the earth erupted. It lasted nearly sixty seconds. Sixty long seconds in which people were violently thrown from their beds and knocked around inside their dwellings. Plaster fell from the ceilings, lights flickered, and glass shattered throughout the city. The quake roared with a ravenous sound, as if to eat everything in its path.

"Thousands of people needed to be rescued. Staircases were destroyed only to leave occupants trapped above them. Others were trapped on stairs while their houses fell around them to rubble. Finally the shaker subsided, and people moved to the windows and out to the streets to survey the damage. San Francisco had been more than shaken; it was now in a shambles. No one knew then, but this quake, with the epicenter two miles out to sea near Mussel Rock, unleashed a measured 7.9–8.3 tremblor that would forever change the lives of, and test the resolve of, its citizens. Like the fire that came shortly after the quake, nature did not discriminate. The city was a mass of ruins. The people, no matter their class, were all paupers now."

"What did people do, Grandpa?"

"Most were disoriented with nowhere to go— probably in shock. Some gathered their families and whatever belongings that remained and left the city with nothing more than the clothes on their backs. Business people found their buildings ablaze or flattened by the quake. Transportation was nonexistent. Delivery wagons that were crammed with goods, when located, went to the highest bidder.

"And then there was the fire. Whether it was fueled by broken gas mains or candles falling over, it devoured the city. The streets welled up, leaving gaping holes. Sidewalks and floors moved like the changing of the tides around Alcatraz. Buildings that appeared to be untouched upon closer examination revealed fire escapes now at sidewalk level. What had once been a four-story structure was now two stories."

"How could so much of a great city be destroyed in one minute?" Luc asked.

Just then the incipient fire in Grandpa's hearth began spitting sparks and growing in size and intensity. The squeezebox swayed on the rocker as it moved back and forth. The bellows began to expand. Renzo and Dante put their heads down between their legs and covered their eyes with their oversized paws.

"What's happening?"

Grandpa stood up and put both hands on Luc's shoulders. "Are you ready, Luc?"

"So soon? I think so! Maybe I should do my homework first?"

Grandpa peered at him over his glasses as if to say, "Really?"

Luc chuckled. "Nah!"

"You need only to put on old Lucky Leather and you're off."

Luc picked up the fire helmet belonging to his grandfather, the one he had played with hundreds of times before. This time he noticed a shield held on by the great brass eagle, showing the insignia of Chemical Company Number 5. He glanced over at the squeezebox, rockin' and rollin' nearby. Then... Crash! Bang! Plop!

Luc found himself in a sand dune on the outskirts of Golden Gate Park and the Western Addition.

"What am I sitting on?" Luc said aloud to no one after being tumbled through time, as if in a washing machine.

"Am I supposed to get used to this? I wonder if I can get frequent-flier miles?" He shuffled around a bit, and realized he had actually landed on a dog's paw.

"Oh, I'm sorry little guy, did I hurt you?" Luc looked closer to find the dog had a squashed face.

"Did I do that?"

The dog gave him a little snarl, then a grunt.

"Oh, you're a bulldog. You already know you're funny lookin'. You have black and white spots like a Dalmatian. "What's your name, buddy?" Luc reached for the collar around his neck buried under the rolls of excess skin. "Says here your name is Brutus. You live at 412 Bush Street." Luc looked around a bit and realized he might be in San Francisco, but this wasn't the city he recognized, or his neighborhood.

"Well, Brutus, my newfound friend, seems we're both lost." Brutus barked, then burped. He did not have the good manners to be embarrassed. The tip of his tongue protruded an inch from the right side of his underbite, and he continued to pant away, his entire body rolling with the tremors of his panting.

"Let's use this app I've got. We can scan your license and it will give me the name of your owners, your address, and directions to where you live." Then he remembered. "Probably no connection here 'cause I can see we're in the past. How did they do it without the Internet?" Luc brushed the sand off his bottom, surveying his surroundings.

"Grandpa always taught navigation to me in case I ever got lost." Luc looked straight up to see the sun going on its downward trajectory.

"Brutus, that's the west, so the opposite direction is toward the city. I think where you come from on Bush Street is to the east. Probably a bit nor'east." Brutus began to bark and waddle toward downtown, sort of gesturing in his own way for Luc to follow.

"You know, Brutus, for a lost dog you sure seem to know exactly where you're going." As they walked, Luc noticed the hazy sky and felt the unusually muggy, humid air. Luc began to feel a sense of trepidation and a sinking feeling in his stomach. He remembered that whenever these conditions existed in San Francisco, its inhabitants referred to it as "earthquake weather." Luc knew he could not stop the inevitable but still wondered what his mission would be on this trip—besides trying to find the amulet.

As Luc and Brutus reached the outskirts of downtown, they encountered more people. Lots of eyes scanned this tall, thin curly blond kid dressed bizarrely compared to the fashion of the day. But here on the Barbary Coast there were all kinds of people from all walks of life. Even in 1906, the people of San Francisco simply accepted other people, no matter how strange or different they seemed.

Luc continued to follow his new friend, who now appeared to be out for an evening stroll rather than lost. They finally reached Bush Street as the sun dipped behind some of the taller buildings. The temperature had cooled to a comfortable level, but it was still warmer than usual. Luc listened to the ever-increasing grunts and groans from Brutus, who had picked up his wheezing along with his pace.

"Must be close, huh fella?"

Brutus darted into what Luc realized was a stable on Bush Street. He was barking like a dog on the attack. Luc looked up to see the fire hall, Chemical Company Number 5, located at 410 and 412 Bush Street. Ding!

Luc's brain popped as he recognized the logo as the same brass eagle from Grandpa's helmet.

Next to the fire hall was the California Hotel. The entire block bustled with people moving in and out of shops and businesses, meeting and greeting, coming and going. It was quite the busy place. The hotel towered over the firehouse with its huge stained glass, shiny brass dome, and chimneys pointing toward the sky.

A huge pumper stood in front on the apron of the firehouse, the engineer tending to its upkeep. The other firefighters worked alongside, ever vigilant, training with the rescue tools of the day. Tools always had to be at the ready.

Brutus, looking like a happy dog indeed, came bounding out of the stables dedicated to the horses that pulled the heavy pumper to emergencies and fires. Following close behind was a large, stout, jovial man in uniform.

"So you must be the latest friend Brutus used to get him home. I'm John Coyne. And you would be?"

"Luc Sullivan, sir."

"Sullivan, ahh! Just what we need: another Sullivan!" He laughed mirthfully, as if he had told a joke. "Where you from boy?"

"The Avenues, sir."

"The Avenues? Where might that be, my peculiar new friend?" Just then bells rang out and everyone jumped to attention. As per their training, the horses made their way out of their stalls and crossed the street to fall in line with the harnesses about to be lowered onto them. The leather harnesses were fastened by the engineer with care and readied for departure. As the horses galloped away, everyone in the streets stopped to watch these protectors of the people proceed with fierce dedication. Luc stood awestruck as he finally experienced what he had only been able to picture in his mind's eye from Grandpa's stories. With everyone gone on the dispatch, Luc once again pondered the cruel reality that was about to come true. It was confusing, as he was ready to help, but still not sure of his mission.

"What to do, Brutus? What to do?"

Night fell on the city, and the firefighters returned with no great stories, just a false alarm. John Coyne again approached Luc.

"Son, since Brutus has brought you all this way, and it's getting late, the least we can do is feed you and put you up here for the night."

"Thank you, sir. That would be great. Sir, how did Brutus get black spots like a Dalmatian?"

"Looks a bit strange, does he? Don't know for certain. I think he always wanted to be a carriage dog, so the spots started to appear. Never gave it much thought. He's actually the chief's dog.

"The chief lives here, too?" Luc asked. "Which chief?"

"THE chief, of course! Dennis Sullivan."

"No way!"

"You're probably related."

John walked away to gather some food for Luc. "Dinner in ten, and if you have any issues tonight, you can ask Maroney over at the station. He's got the night watch." "Dinner in ten" reminded Luc of meals at home with Mom and Dad.

"Brutus, I wish tomorrow would never come. I feel so helpless. No one would listen to me anyway. After dinner, we have to try and sleep. We'll be workin' tomorrow." Luc saw a spot in the loft, full of hay. It looked lofty but poky.

Luc tossed and turned into the night. He dreamed of the events that would soon take place, as he had already vividly explored them through Grandpa's stories.

At 5:30 A.M, April 18, 1906, Luc awoke to the barking and slobbering of Brutus, whose front paws were perched on his chest. Luc sprang from his spot. "Is it time?"

Brutus rolled over several times trying to tell Luc something. He was trying to tell him that he had missed it, slept through the whole thing.

Luc ran to the opening of the large double doors of the stables and stopped in his tracks, his eyes wide open. The dust was still settling from the quake. All the horses from the stables were bucking and running in circles, eyes wild. As he focused through the dust, he could see where, just hours before, Chemical Company Number 5 had stood three stories high. Now it lay in ruins. Luc did not know what to do, so he ran to the side of firefighters who stood in front of what was left of the fire hall. Some were on their knees digging; others were ferrying away debris. He could see John Coyne managing the scene.

"Mr. Coyne, what can I do to help?"

"We need all hands, my boy. The chief and his wife are trapped, and others at the station are still not accounted for. How can we help the city if we don't have all our men? We also need some large lengths of wood to help shore up our path into the hall."

Luc knew exactly what Coyne was referring to and started gathering the proper materials.

"Luc," Coyne cautioned, "be careful of the California Hotel next door. Its dome is what gave way and fell onto the station, taking it down. The hotel is not stable. It could come down any minute."

"Yes, sir."

Luc continued to search out more wood, with his head on a swivel while he surveyed the buildings. Luc looked up to see that the brick façade of the hotel was crumbling. Guests were running, with nowhere to go except into the streets. They had nothing more on than the nightclothes they had been wearing. Luc surveyed the collapse patterns on the firehouse and could tell that the dome had fallen directly through the center of the roof and had not stopped until it reached the apparatus floor. Luc sized up the situation and realized that on either side of the hole, the bearing walls had been sucked into each other. This left certain V-shaped voids on all floors, increasing the chance to save the chief, his wife, and the missing firefighters. Luc tried to update Captain Coyne on his findings, only to have the captain redirect his efforts to another location.

"Son, you need to clear everyone out of the hotel and size up the rear of the firehouse. If we get stalled here, or we get more help, we can come at it another way. For now, this is what we got to do. Survey and report back."

Luc grabbed some rope and an ax from the stables and made his way into the California Hotel. He pretty much did not have to tell people twice to leave. The hotel was devastated. The only thing left was the creaking and groaning of the bones of the building that were trying to keep from falling on him and Brutus. Luc reached the back windows on the fifth floor corner and looked down to see that the walls of the fire hall had pulled away and in, toward themselves, to the center at a 45-degree angle. Yet the walls were still intact. He was also able to get a 360-degree view of the city from up there.

There was an awesome reality in the sheer destruction. Fires burned all over the city, and they were beginning to march toward each other, combining and moving closer together.

"Time to pick it up, Brutus. We've got to get in there and save the chief and his wife and whoever else is trapped."

Luc moved to the hotel's third floor and decided to move around the corner to the collapsing sidewall of the station. When he reached the third-floor rear window, he realized he needed more tools and a strategy.

"Okay Brutus, let's check my rescue app for some ideas. Luckily, I kept these things on the desktop in case I ever needed them."

Luc reviewed the data on his phone, thankful these were downloads and did not require Wi-Fi, and identified items in the hotel that might be substituted for tools. He turned his attention outside the window.

"Brutus, here's the plan. I think once we get onto the collapsed wall, we can breach that wall into the void that's been created. Due to the failure of the center supports, there seem to be two identifiable voids. Now we need to locate a good anchor spot for a rope-tie here in the room." Luc continued to think out loud before he realized Brutus was barking and sitting on a large couch.

"Great idea, Brutus! We'll use the couch. You're a smart dog." Luc moved the couch to the window and wrapped the rope around it three times, securing the tensionless hitch. Then he took his ax, pickside, and opened above the window so he could run the line through while having a higher point to work from inside the window. To balance the rope, he threw it around the corner and onto the collapsed portion of the wall he intended to descend upon. Luc took a position, standing in the window, tied off to his cool belt buckle—the one that doubled as a carabiner—made from rescue webbing.

Brutus cocked his head with curiosity. Luc took his ax, reached around the corner, and plunged it into the wall. He tore away at it to create a purchase, or space, for his eventual toehold, as well as one for his hands. After a couple of blows he holstered the ax in his belt and reached for Brutus.

"Come on, Brutus, time to go." Brutus let out a snort and a grumble and backed off.

"Guess that's a no. Okay, see ya when I see ya."

Luc swung around and took hold of the purchase points. Then he looped the bite of the rope up and over an attachment protruding from the siding above. That gave him the change of direction that allowed him to repel without swinging back and missing the building all together.

Luc was making his first repel when he heard barking below. He continued to push off the wall for his final descent and saw Brutus waiting there panting and barking.

"Brutus how, what? Where...? Oh, forget it! Glad you're here, buddy."

Luc proceeded to locate the best spot to open up and make entrance, knowing full well that his efforts could be too late. He still had plenty of rope to get down into the building and out, but what was below? Luc opened the roof with his ax, breaking through the siding and subsequently the lath and plaster of the interior wall. As he opened up the hole large enough to enter, he saw large amounts of debris creating obstacles he would have to deal with one at a time. The biggest obstacle was the broken steamlines throughout the building. Now that the wall was open, the only sound you could hear was the screaming whistle of the steam escaping the hot-water sources.

"Not quite sure where the steam is, so stay close," Luc told Brutus, fully aware of the danger.. "Can't let the steam hit us, or we'll be fried."

He then performed a primary search of the void he had entered and saw it was all clear. "Down to the next floor Brutus." Brutus started barking from across what was left of that floor.

"Brutus, you're quick. You found some stairs? Wait, those aren't stairs. It's some kind of slide. No, it's a chute to send coal from floor to floor for the stoves." Luc had listened closely to Grandpa's stories. And Brutus seemed to get everything he was saying. That dog was uncanny. Or maybe Luc himself was losing his mind during all these travels to perilous times.

"Brutus, I get the feeling you're more than a dog and you understand me. What's up with that?"

Without waiting for an answer, Luc threw the rope down the hole to the next floor. This time he grabbed Brutus and wrapped him up with one arm, while he grasped the rope with the other and slid down the coal hole. Luc looked at his new sidekick.

"Got you now." As they slipped down, the hiss of the leaking steam grew dangerously close. The only noise that interfered with the steam sound was an obnoxious ringtone alerting Luc that his battery was losing its charge. Luc reached the landing below and silenced the built-in alarm. He looked at Brutus, who was covering his little ears with his paws.

"Come on now, Brutus, that's the latest coolest ringtone. Got it online with my iTunes gift card." Through a cloud of dust, Luc could see that the floor they were now on had definitely been living quarters. With Brutus in one hand and the rope in the other, Luc was able to swing across the floor and not lose his bearings.

They both heard groaning sounds coming from beyond their reach. Brutus broke free and hightailed it toward the sounds of life.

"Brutus, whatcha got?" Brutus's little stub of a tail was wagging with his butt following close behind as he stood in front of a pile of bricks, barking and nudging the pile with his nose. The dog had recognized two people trapped, with steam roaring above their heads. It was probably Chief Sullivan and his wife.

"Good... dog,... Brutus," the chief groaned, clearly in pain. "You brought help."

Luc asserted his presence with confidence. "Chief, I'm here to get you and your wife out. Let's get this rubble off of you and stop the bleeding from that gash on your head."

Luc began administering first aid and life support to the victims, when suddenly everything began to shake.

"It's an aftershock, cover up!" Luc jumped to protect the chief and wife and dragged Brutus in with them. It was a big one, as it felt like the longest five seconds ever. Dust filled the air as the tremor subsided, again rearranging the room and rubble. Brutus made his way through the debris searching for life among the wreckage.

"Whatcha got, pal?" Luc yelled. "One more over there?"

With the aftershock subsiding, the chief had been shaken free of the rubble and was tending to his wife. Luc made his way to Brutus and came upon a firefighter trapped by a huge beam that lay across his lower body. Luc would need a lever and a fulcrum. He yelled over to the chief.

"Chief, I've got one of your men here. He's trapped, but I can get him free." Luc now had two rescues in the making, so the back and forth began. With the steam blowing down in the direction of the chief, there was no alternative but to sacrifice himself momentarily to the steam to recover his wife.

The firefighter was now stabilized. Luc continued his double duty, grabbing the first shield-like object he came upon. He used thick bedding to cover himself as he made his way to help shelter the chief from the fierce steam. Luc and the chief freed Mrs. Sullivan and pulled her to the side, where she lay unconscious.

"Stand by, I'll be right back." Luc now doubled back and on his way saw a large brass bedpost about six feet high and three inches in diameter.

"Perfect lever. Now I need a good fulcrum."

Luc eyed a pile of bricks and stacked them just a few feet back from the lift, then shimmied the lever over the stack and under the load.

"How're you doing under there, sir?"

"I'll be a tad better when I'm free of this."

Luc maneuvered the lever and put all his weight into it, just budging the load.

"Quick, Brutus! Get aboard and put something into it with me!" Straddled with his stubby legs and as best he could, Brutus put his weight on the top of the lever once, then again. With a bit more effort, the firefighter pulled himself free.

"Thank you, lad. You saved my life. What's your name?"

"Luc, Luc Sullivan." The fireman began to laugh.

"Seems to me the only ones stuck in this place are Sullivans."

"You mean you're a Sullivan, too?"

"You bet I am. But no relation; from the same county in the old country we are. How about you?"

"I don't think so."

Luc dwelled on the oddity for only a second before he was interrupted by another aftershock—this time, longer than the last.

"Quickly, over to the coal chute. It's the only way." Luc ordered. The men gathered up the chief's wife. Luc placed the rope down and formed a hasty harness to secure the unconscious woman for lowering. Firefighter Sullivan got the chief ready. Suddenly the room began to fill with smoke. The California Hotel was now ablaze, causing a deep haze. In the back of the smoke, Luc sighted that same green spot, lingering just out of reach. Barely noticing, Luc forged ahead with Brutus, and his rescued party continued. The chief was now beside his wife and ready for their descent. They slowly made their way down the coal-laden tunnel to the safety of the receptive rescuers coming from the other direction. Desperately in need of medical attention, the chief exited from the pile on two feet, while his wife was carried off in the direction of the hospital. Luc felt relieved he had accomplished his mission, a mission that just moments before he had no idea would be his to achieve. Luc turned his attention to Firefighter Sullivan.

"It's your turn now, sir," Luc said. All the while the smoke banked down to a level where both were forced to suck what little air was left from the floor. The bottom of the coal chute acted like an inverted chimney as the smoke poured out.

"You know, young Sullivan, your bravery saved the chief and his wife. I was attempting the same thing when this beam came crashing down. You saved me as well, and I thank you."

"Not quite finished yet. Maybe we should get a move on."

Sullivan, who seemed strangely familiar, asked Luc as they moved to the chute, "Who taught you about the lever and the fulcrum and those fancy knots?" Luc looked at the man, then to his smartphone alarm indicating a dead battery.

At the same instance, there was another aftershock. The California Hotel was now fully engulfed in flames, and the wood-framed, brick-faced building was giving in, collapsing onto the hopeless remains of the fire-house known as Chemical Company Number 5. Just as Luc followed Sullivan down the chute, the speed made him fade into the time conveyor. He started his tumble home, echoing behind him: "My Graaaaandpa taught me... Wait! It's youuuuu!"

As Luc felt himself get sucked into the vortex, he realized he was not alone. At the last second, his new buddy Brutus must have fallen in alongside him. Luc had saved the chief and his wife, and the thought that he might have saved his Grandpa, too, was blowing his mind.

Crash! Bang! Plop!

Chapter Nine

GOOD TO SEE YOU AGAIN, LUC. THANKS FOR BACKING me up in there." Grandpa said.

"I thought I had this stuff figured out, and then you showed up. I didn't realize it was you till... How could it be? Why didn't you keep the chief and his wife safe? And why didn't you tell me before that you would be there...?"

"Thought it might be easier to explain after you had the experience." Grandpa turned to look at the dog. "Hello, Brutus, nice to see you're in fine shape after the trip." Brutus barked a couple of times, then waddled up for a scratch.

"Brutus is yours now, Luc. He'll be your steadfast traveling companion, and you can trust he'll always be by your side."

"What about the chief? Brutus belongs to him, and they'll be looking for him." Grandpa walked over to Luc and put a hand on his shoulder, looking directly into his eyes.

"Luc, I'm sorry. The chief didn't live."

"I saw them walk out! He was alive! I saved him... and his wife!" Grandpa sat Luc down on the sofa. Brutus nudged up next to them.

"His injuries were very serious. Four days later he died, though his wife did survive."

Luc lowered his head.

"I know you're upset. Regardless, you *did* save them. Things happen for a reason, Luc. That's the special meaning of history. After his death, the City of San Francisco accomplished many things in his name."

"Why, Grandpa?"

"It's okay, Luc. You thought your mission was to save the chief. Well, your mission was actually to save me, and in doing so you have preserved history."

"Since I saved you... then you were able to have a family and have Dad, who then had me, right? But if I wasn't around yet, how could I come back to save you if I hadn't been born yet?"

Grandpa gave a chuckle. "Luc, the power you've been entrusted with—time travel rescue—defies all reasonable intelligence. The genius required lies beyond rational thought and requires a higher degree of intelligence." Grandpa glanced at the bust on the bookshelf. "Like Florian before you, this remarkable power given to you is based on your faith in the greater good. Go with it. Embrace the adventure."

"Oh yeah, this out-of-place green something keeps appearing in the smoke, is that..."

"Luc, the mystery of today will gradually be solved over time. Then you will know. As I have told you before, a bit at a time, a bit at a time."

"Maybe I'm not the right guy." Luc said.

"No, you are indeed," Grandpa said.

"Along with saving my friend's ancestors, what else could I possibly need to do? And what about clues to solve the mystery? When do I get those?"

"You've already had two adventures knowing your ties to Florian, Luc. Maybe there are clues within those rescues, maybe not. But it's time for dinner. You ought to be getting home."

"Yeah, clues, I think..." Luc said, reaching for more.

"Later, my boy"

Grandpa walked Luc to the front door. "Say hello to your mom and dad. And, Luc, I think it's best to keep this between us right now. Brutus can sleep here."

"Okay, Grandpa." Luc bounded down the steps, flushed with excitement once again. Grandpa's old saying "Every day's a new adventure" suddenly had new meaning.

Chapter Ten

RENZO, DANTE, BRUTUS! COME ON, BOYS! COOKIES!" Luc shouted. The three dogs came sliding around the corner of the dining room, their nails slipping and sliding and doing everything to get to Luc first while at the same time keeping on their feet.

"Good dogs! Okay, settle, settle. Hey, where's Brutus?" Suddenly Brutus was right next to him, as if he had just appeared out of nowhere.

"How the heck did you get there? Hey, where are your Dalmatian spots?"

"Not sure why, but they tend to disappear when he comes back to present day," Grandpa said as he entered the kitchen.

"Love to give the boys treats. Hope you don't mind, Grandpa."

"That's just fine, but not too many. Dante and Brutus are getting a little porky." Both dogs cranked their heads toward Grandpa. Luc could have sworn he could see Renzo grinning.

"Luc, we've talked about the legend of Florian, and you asked about clues to solving the mystery. Before your next adventure, you must realize that you have more to do than just protect history, and at times, your friends' ancestors. Along with those noble rescues, you'll be charged with seeking out a very important element that has been lost. When returned to its proper place, this element will stabilize the power we share, allowing all of us to better control our destinies."

"What is the element, Grandpa? An amulet like the one Florian wore around his neck when they killed him?"

"Precisely! It's a piece of the large stone used to drown Florian when fire could not harm him. After he drowned, the stone transformed to an emerald-like stone. The amulet is jagged-cut, green, and encrusted in a gold Maltese iron firefighters' cross with a large chain."

"How could you lose that?"

Grandpa tilted his head with a grin. "First, Luc, you must continue to travel and do your duty. Second, legend has it that to recapture and harness the amulet, you must follow a sequence of clues. The closer you get, the more you'll see it. The more you see it, the more you'll know it's within your reach. But the sequence that must be followed is difficult. You must complete your rescue before seizing the amulet. If not completed in sequence, the amulet will fade, and you must begin again."

"You said that all in one breath, and I'm still holding mine. Doesn't sound very easy. I mean, the rescues were already pretty tight time-wise and kinda sketchy maneuver-wise, and now this? I'm not exactly sure of what you mean. Is the amulet an object or like a vision?"

"Both. It is a vision that crystallizes the closer you get."

"And then you grab it?"

"You reach for it. But if you stop any part of the rescue sequence, it will disappear."

"So I have to figure out how to continue the rescue *and* reach for it at the same time."

"Luc, it's never been done before now. All we know is that it must be done, and you're the one who's been entrusted to save the family."

"Save the family! What do you mean?"

"The amulet was released during a rescue and then lost."

"Where did you lose it?"

"I didn't lose it, your father did."

"You told me that Dad wanted nothing to do with this."

"Yes. That's what he said after his greatest loss—the loss of his partner. Your father was and is a great fire-fighting soldier. He exemplifies Florian in all regards. But on that day, your father and his partner were in deep—deeper than most firefighters ever venture into a fire. They knew that a baby was trapped, along with other firefighters. So they crawled down the hallway on the third floor with fire everywhere out of control."

Luc sat in awe as he listened to this account of heroism—one he had never heard from his father.

"The two men had already located a downed fire-fighter and dragged him to the second-floor landing before returning to the search. They could hear a crying baby in the distance. There was no breathing apparatus in those days, just leather lungs to get the job done. They both sucked air off the ground and some from windows as they passed. As they moved down the hallway and into one of the rooms, the fire closed in behind them leaving them no retreat. They got to the screaming baby inside the room and knew that their only exit was the light well.

"Your father's partner was anxious to keep moving and shimmied out the window first, calling for the baby. Right then, your father felt the amulet around his neck fading into the smoke. His partner fell from his purchase backward, down into the light well and to his death.

"Still in danger with the baby in his arms, your dad felt a bitter jolt to his system—the unfairness of it all. With no time to respond, your father was able to make it to another window where a ladder awaited. The baby was saved, but your father lost faith."

Luc sat there in disbelief. He thought of how hurt his father must have been. How he had shouldered this loss for all these years? He himself had privately misjudged his father for not embracing the power of rescue travel his father had offered to him years ago.

"Grandpa, why did the power fail Dad? Why didn't it save both the baby and his partner?"

"Oh, Luc, I have been asking and searching for the answer to that question since the day it happened. All I can say is that some things just happen for reasons we can't understand.

"The amulet and the legend let your father down that day, after so many other great rescues in the past. Your father has never forgiven or forgotten and has never revisited the power of rescue travel. The amulet has resurfaced in your adventures. That is why you must recapture it."

"Grandpa, I think one of the clues presented itself during my rescue of Will's great-great-grandmother."

"Did you see the amulet on that trip?"

"You know I did... I mean I *think* I did." Luc scratched his head trying to remember.

"When I was on the ladder securing his mother to the rope, in the background below—in the light well—I saw what looked like a reflection in one of the lower windows. The building was ready to explode. But for just an instant, I thought I saw a small bright green object/spot from within the fire, reflected in the window. I didn't have any time to think about it then. But, yes, I think it was the amulet showing itself to me. Grandpa, that's a clue, right? I thought I saw it in the burning light well."

"Luc, your father's partner perished in a light well."

Luc walked home pondering how his father must have shouldered that burden all these years. Somehow, he had misread his dad's position. The more he walked, the more Luc felt he had done his father a great disservice in thinking Joseph Sullivan was somehow derelict in his duties as a firefighter. He knew his father was always good, great even in Luc's eyes. But it was not until this moment that Luc realized a true hero is one who acts without accolades. Any anguish is always theirs alone to carry. With duty comes that burden in the fire service.

Chapter Eleven

LUC HOPPED UP THE STEPS TO THE BACK DOOR AND flung open the door into the kitchen, moving straight to the fridge.

"Hi, Mom, what's for dinner?" His mom came in from the other room to see Luc with his head buried deep inside the refrigerator.

"Nothing new in there since the last time you looked this morning, at lunch, and for a snack an hour later. You're wearing the hinges off on the door." Luc bumped his head as he pulled it out to look at his mom's face.

"Seriously?" She had that look moms get when they're all proud of taking care of you and watching you grow up and all that.

"Before you get comfortable, young man, take a look on that chair there." Luc pulled it out from under the table to find a tool belt with nails, screws, a hammer, and a screwdriver.

"Those aren't mine."

"Well, they're yours now so you don't have to borrow your dad's. It'll help you finish fixing the fence you tore down.

"But..."

"You just get your butt into the backyard and help your father, who has spent the last two hours fixing the damage from your infamous 'rescue.' I think he could use a hand."

Luc groaned and grabbed the tools, heading for the backyard. He *had* been negligent the last few days, what with all the time travel. He got home pretty late from Grandpa's, and sometimes while he was a bit tired from the rescue, his thoughts were more exhausting.

"Hey, Luc! You guys really did a number on this fence. I haven't gotten very far, but... we'll get it."

Luc relaxed, seeing his dad wasn't mad about the fence. "What can I do? Can I get you more wood from the garage?"

"That can wait. I need a break." They both sat on the lawn.

"See Grandpa today?"

"Yeah, he's good."

"Dogs?"

"Yeah, good too."

"Any good stories?"

"Yeah, you know Grandpa..."

There was a brief silence. Luc looked at his dad. He could see it in his eyes. "You know, don't you?"

"I've always known, Luc. That's part of the power."

"I thought you left it behind."

"I left it, but it didn't leave me. Residual power still calls on me occasionally."

"Your partner... I'm so sorry Dad. I didn't know, I—I..."

"It's okay, Luc, you know now. And the way you feel has made it a little better in my heart." Joe put his arm around his son. "Time, my boy, time."

Luc could see the change in his father, like someone had lightened his load.

Mom's voice sailed through an upstairs window. "Dinner at 18:30! Sharp!"

Luc stood up and reached out to help his dad stand. Joe looked at the fence and the hedge, scratching his head under his baseball cap.

"Say, Luc, what were you guys doing again?"

"Well, right out of the manual... Telford line slash zip-line rescue egress."

"Are you kidding me? I'm surprised you both aren't in the hospital." Dad got a sly grin on his face. "Let's do this right."

"The fence?"

"No, the rescue."

Luke could not believe his ears. "Wh-what about Mom?"

"No worries, I'm a professional." The guys sneaked up on the back porch. Dad worked fast, re-rigging the cable and checking the anchor, which was still hooked into Mrs. Martin's window frame on the other end. Luc and his dad put on makeshift harnesses and got up on the railing.

"Are you sure about this?" Luc asked.

"Yeah, we'll have some fun before we fix everything."

Suddenly Mom opened the sliding glass door, startling them. "Okay, Sullivan boys, what..."

But it was too late. Luc and his dad were already tumbling through the air with no way to control their descent—no friction at all! Within seconds they had taken out the new section of the fence as they both fell into the hedge. Joe ended up on Mrs. Martin's side. As he raised himself up and brushed himself off, he came eye to eye with Mrs. M herself, who stood there with her arms crossed, smoking mad. She glanced at Luc struggling to get out of the bushes, then looked at the SFFD insignia on Joe's baseball cap.

"I hope there aren't any more of you Sullivans protecting this city, or we're in big trouble." Mrs. Martin turned on her heels and marched back into her house.

Mom, who had been watching everything from the back door, could not help but bust out laughing. She covered her mouth quickly and tried to greet the boys with a mighty stern look but then practically spit on her hands she was laughing so hard.

"Clear now where you get it from, Luc Sullivan," she giggled. Then she set her sights on her husband. "Not exactly very smart of you, is it now, Captain Sullivan?"

Luc and his father ran inside the door without even trying to hide their laughter, which had now escalated into guffaws.

Mom had the last word. "Go wash up for dinner, the both of you." Luc hightailed it to the bathroom while Joe used the kitchen sink. He washed his hands and splashed water on his face, only to see his wife standing next to him. She handed him a towel and got close to his ear. She whispered, "You talked to him about it, didn't you?"

"I did."

She kissed him on the cheek, trying to hide her emotions.

"How did *you* know?" Joe asked.

"Some of your Celtic gift just might have rubbed off on me as well."

He looked at her curiously.

"Actually, I was listening from the upstairs window. Now go check on your son and make sure he isn't hurt, Captain."

Joe made his way to the bathroom to find Luc dabbing a superficial cut on his arm.

"Here, son, let me take a look at that." They continued their father/son discussion while finishing their cleanup.

Luc's dad spoke freely. "Son, knowing you are taking over the reins has helped me... let go of some of my... hurt from my partner's death. I feel somehow like I've renewed my spirit. Like a personal milestone I didn't understand how much I had to reach. I don't feel... haunted anymore. That's why I got so silly today with you. I feel young again."

Luc smiled. "Don't push it, Dad. It's not like you're all that young!"

His dad clocked him on the arm—the other one.

"Rescue travel rocks!" said Luc. "Admit it."

His dad put his arm around Luc's shoulder. "It sure does, son. It sure does."

Dinner was awesome as usual. "Fine meal, my dear."

"Thank you kindly, sir."

"Luc, there's still some daylight out there. Want to toss the old pigskin around?"

Luc jumped up and was out the door in a flash. He was so excited to have this time with his father, not to mention a moment to show Dad new football skills.

"I've got to warm up a bit, so take it easy." Dad said.

But Luc was already moving farther away, firing spirals in Dad's direction.

Joe quickly hit his stride. "I'm sure your Grandpa has spoken about Florian."

"Can't help like what that guy is all about. Really cool."

"And the amulet? What do you think?" Dad asked. Luc was in awe of the fact that his father was speaking about time travel so openly. "The stone, Luc, is and always will be a part of us. Florian, too. This emerald-like stone is what we are about. The fire service—now, then, and forever. But there are challenges you need to understand as you go forward."

"You sound like Grandpa. What else is there to know?"

"Grandpa's nature is to not tell you everything, but to guide you enough so you can figure it out for yourself."

As Luc listened, he began to feel uneasy about the amulet. He felt bad about the fact that he did not quite believe Grandpa and Dad's explanation of it. He was completely loyal to the both of them and in the past had never questioned their beliefs. But now, as his own man, he found he was questioning everybody's beliefs as he searched for his own meaning of things—especially something as mysterious as the amulet.

Chapter Twelve

Ah, Luc, you're just in time. Whatcha doin'?"

"Coming to see you after football practice."

"Good workout?"

"Yep. What's up, Grandpa?"

"I need help putting the wood and coal up for the winter. A San Francisco summer can chill you to the bone."

"You're done, Grandpa. I'll bring up the rest for you."

"Thanks, Luc. Many a hand makes light work." Grandpa sat on the steps of his grand old house and reached for his perfectly ironed handkerchief to wipe his brow. "It takes six months to dry that wood before it's ready for the fireplace."

"Why not just turn on the heater?"

"Nah." Grandpa quipped, doing a perfect imitation of Luc, who was running up and down the steps with his arms wrapped around six logs at a time.

"Okay, break time's over for me."

"No, Grandpa, I got this."

"Luc, never ask anyone to do anything you wouldn't do yourself."

Just as Grandpa reached the bottom of the steps, he was greeted by his next-door neighbor. "Hi, Captain Sullivan!"

"Hello Amelia, and how are we today?"

"Fine, thanks. Do you need help?"

"Why, yes, thank you kindly. One more set of strong arms can only help."

Luc could swear Grandpa saw him shake his head "Nooo!" at the top of the steps but just chose to ignore him. He ducked into the front door with his arms full of wood, hoping against hope that she would just go away.

Amelia was the same age as he, with an abundance of long, curly auburn hair and startling blue eyes. "Is Luc here?" she asked his grandfather.

Luc could hear the chuckle all the way up the steps. "Luc, me boy?" Grandpa glanced over his shoulder to see a reluctant Luc acknowledging Amelia with a nod and a weak wave. "Hello."

Luc actually liked Amelia. They were in the same class, so he saw her all the time anyway. But this was supposed to be his guy time with Grandpa. More importantly, Luc was now on a mission to retrieve the amulet, and that certainly did not involve Amelia.

Grandpa bridged the awkward moment. "I believe we're good for the day. Let's get a treat and something to drink. It's the least I can do to thank you both for helping out." He started up the stairs with Renzo and Dante not too far behind.

"C'mon, Brutus, you too." Urging the fireplug of a dog to his feet, Grandpa made it into the kitchen, where he got three glasses out of the cupboard and a pitcher of lemonade from the fridge.

"Luc, I think it's time for a story."

"Uh, not right now Grandpa..." Luc said, indicating Amelia with a tilt of his head.

"Luc! We can *all* share a story."

Luc could not *believe* this. Grandpa was about to blow it!

Grandpa grabbed the plate of cookies before moving to the living room with his two young assistants and the three dogs, who were eyeing the cookies hopefully. He sat on the edge of his big chair and reached for his ropes. Tying knots helped him relax.

"Grandpa, check this out," Luc began. "I've been practicing the one you showed me... Figure eight with a loop." Luc proceeded as he described his mastery. "Take a bight, make a bend, twist bight with left hand, bring lower loop up through, clean it up, and finish with a safety one inch from the knot. Bingo! Perfect. Whatcha think?"

"That is a fine figure eight knot, Luc," Grandpa said, examining the rope.

Luc stood up proudly, then grimaced, reaching for his knees.

"Knees sore from football?"

"Nope."

"Captain Sullivan?" interrupted Amelia. "Can I show you the knot you taught me?"

"Absolutely."

"It's the butterfly knot."

Luc stopped short in shock. The butterfly? *She* knew the butterfly?

"Okay," Amelia began. "Rope in palm of hand, one complete wrap, then another in between the first two. Pull wrap closest to fingertips out and back toward the thumb, then put under wraps going back toward fingertips. Tighten and clean it up. Voilà! A pretty butterfly!"

"Excellent, Amelia. Good job!" Grandpa said.

Luc thought he might barf right then and there.

"Pretty butterfly?" he muttered to himself.

"What's that, Luc?" Grandpa asked, examining Amelia's rope.

"I have to be home by 6:00 for dinner. Plenty of time for an adven—a story." *What could it hurt?* Luc thought. It was not like he would be able to transport through time with a *girl* in the room. So why not? "Go for it, Grandpa."

Amelia and the dogs looked at him curiously, but Grandpa was already beginning the story. "There have been many great fires in history but never one with so much lore attached to it. And never one that has caused so much ruckus as to how or who started it. It was October 8th on the south side of Chicago. Eighteen seventy-one was the year. It was around eight o'clock at night, and it hadn't rained for weeks.

"During those days, Chicago was a city made out of wood and the fastest-growing city in the United States. Blocks and blocks of dry and brittle construction wood lay in piles, ripe for fire. That's not to say they hadn't already had their share that season. The fire departments were staffed with tired men who were praying for rain. And on that day, there was thunder and lightning, but no rain in sight.

"Patrick and Catherine O'Leary lived at 137 De Koven Street in two small cottages with an adjacent barn. Inside the barn were their three cows, Daisy, Madeline, and Gwendolyn."

"Those are cute names for cows," Amelia said.

Luc rolled his eyes. "Go on, Grandpa."

"Catherine O'Leary was awakened from a sound sleep by the thunder overhead and the restlessness of her cows, not the party roaring from the front cottage at the McLaughlins'. She took a wrap and a lantern to check on her animals. As she entered the barn, she knew something was amiss. Daisy was out of her stall, mooing and kicking. Gwendolyn and Madelyn began to follow suit. During that very week, the barn had been packed with wood and coal for the upcoming winter. Catherine, who had a true way with animals, approached Daisy to calm her down. As she reached to soothe her, Gwendolyn threw a kick to the rear, launching the lit lantern into the air. With that, in almost slow motion, the Great Chicago Fire began." Grandpa paused.

"Keep going, Grandpa!" begged Luc.

"Quiet, Luc," Grandpa instructed. He was looking at Amelia, who had inexplicably dozed off using the other sleeping beauty, Brutus, for a pillow. Grandpa began to smile. "Must be that all-star softball team she's on. She said she pitched three straight games, back to back today."

"C'mon, please, Grandpa!"

"Luc, look behind you." The Greek fire in the hearth began sparking. The rocker swayed, and Grandma's squeezebox exhaled.

"Luc, it's time. Remember, the amulet cannot be secured without a successful rescue. Use your good sense, follow your heart, adapt as you see fit."

"But Grandpa... what if she—"

"You know more now than ever before. Now don Lucky Leather and have at it, my boy."

As Luc fitted the helmet, the conveyor opened, and he immediately began to tumble through time. During this instantaneous process, he could see nothing, but he loved the feeling of weightlessness. Crash! Bang! Plop!

Luc suddenly appeared on the other end. As usual, he was disheveled at best and always surprised to learn where his rear-end had landed. But this time he had a good idea. Luc looked around.

"I must be in Mrs. O'Leary's barn." He turned his head and gasped. There sat Amelia and Brutus in a pile of hay.

"How did you get here?" They must have been too close to the conveyor. He could understand Brutus, but Amelia? The waves of the time travel vortex had probably simply corralled them all with its energy.

Amelia sat up, her mouth wide open, speechless for a change, thought Luc. Words began to dribble from her mouth. "But where... how did...?" She could not complete her sentences.

"Amelia, I'll tell you later. But for now just follow me." Brutus cuddled up to Luc.

"Thanks for your help, pal, letting her come along and all." Brutus whined and put a paw over his right eye. At least the dog had the sense to be apologetic.

Luc went right to work assessing his surroundings. Just then Catherine O'Leary's lantern landed on a cross beam in the rafters. Mrs. O'Leary entered that area of the barn in hot pursuit of her light source, only to find the three unexpected visitors.

"Now who might you be, and what are you doing in my barn?" Just as the last word was spoken, the lantern was jarred loose from its perch in the rafters by the cows nudging the side beams.

The lantern fell into Luc's lap as he responded to Mrs. O'Leary. "Just here to catch the lantern, Mrs. O'Leary. Thought we could be of some help." Luc, secure in his response, stood up proudly only to notice smoke coming from the stored piles of wood and coal.

"Look over there, smoke!" Brutus ran over to investigate further and began to bark, whining at the extension of fire into the hay.

"It's beginning to roll. Everyone out, now! We've got to get water and alert the fire brigade. Amelia, get to the front cottage where the McLaughlins are having the party and gather them to form a bucket brigade." Amelia paused only for a second, then dashed off in a sprint.

Luc knelt down to Brutus's eye level. "Here's your chance to do some Dalmatian work. Herd those cows to safety upwind so they're not in the path of the fire."

Mrs. O'Leary began to panic. "Oh my Lordy Lord, what now?"

Luc grabbed her shoulders. "That last bolt of dry lightning must have pierced through the roof. We have to make sure everyone is safe first, and we need to alert the fire department."

Luc ran off to the nearest street box, but it was out of service, as was the second, and the third. He tore back to the barn, where he found the bucket brigade working feverishly. The fire had begun to gain strength due to the whipping winds.

"We need more water! There's not enough to keep up. And we better consider moving back to save the cottages. The barn is lost."

The bucket brigade reluctantly turned to face Luc. Luc could only imagine what they thought of him and Amelia, a girl, both in jeans and sneakers. But it was finally his air of authority and sense of command that they responded to. Amelia even straightened her shoulders and moved toward him in support.

"Amelia, I need to go for help. Something's wrong with this delayed response. You stay here with Brutus and make sure they hold their ground against the cottages. Get the roofs first and then soak the perimeter. Can you do that?"

"I've got it covered."

"Cool," said Luc, the approval in his voice giving her even more confidence. Somehow he trusted she would do what was right.

Luc headed north on Fullerton when he realized he should check his phone charge. It was registering, but low, making the urgency of the situation even more intense. He had started to make the connection between his phone charge getting low and the window of the rescue coming to a close. Even though he was moving quickly, he could feel the radiant heat from behind him. Looking south, he could see the expansive glow of the now out-of-control fire. He thought of Amelia and Brutus. He hesitated for a moment, weighed his options, then began to head back to get them before finding a fire station. Human life always comes first. His dad had taught him that.

As he retraced his steps back down Fullerton, he noticed spot fires springing up from the wind-whipped embers. Citizens were fleeing north along with livestock and galloping horses in their wake. Everywhere Luc turned, flames, heat, and smoke filled the streets. The speed of the growing fire was frightening, and the potential devastation seemed insurmountable. Luc stopped to clear his eyes. He tried to get a second wind before continuing on to find his friends. Just as he spun around to get his bearings, he tripped on Brutus, who sat there all browned with smoke.

"Brutus, where's Amelia?"

"C'mon, Sully, we've got work to do!" Amelia cried as she stepped through the smoky haze.

Luc smiled broadly, then returned to the task at hand. "We've got to get to the watchman and let him know that the main fire is here, not where they originally thought it was."

Luc pivoted and pointed toward City Hall. "There!"

Amelia headed off in another direction, running west on Halstead toward the river.

"Amelia, where are you going?"

"Mrs. O'Leary said there was a working alarm box at the pharmacy up the block."

"Okay, then meet me at City Hall!" Luc shouted.

Amelia waved over her shoulder.

"Brutus, stay with Amelia and make sure she gets back to meet me."

Brutus looked at Luc and heaved a heavy sigh. In a flash, lumbering sideways as if his side legs were his front, he caught up to the sprinting Amelia. Luc ran at breakneck speed toward City Hall and the Cook County Courthouse. He could see the fire had now jumped the river and was headed north. Rounding the corner, he found the State Street Bridge totally engulfed in flames.

Now stopped in his tracks, Luc reacted instantly to the problem and backtracked toward the pharmacy, trying to catch up with Amelia and Brutus.

Amelia was waiting for him. "Forgot about the river and burning bridges, didn't ya?"

Brutus put a paw over his eye again. "Oh, so you're an expert now?"

The pharmacy owner was listening to them bicker and interrupted. "You can find a boat down the street at the edge of the river in the trees. I hide it there for fishin' on Sundays. Take it. You'll get there faster."

"Thank you, sir."

"And please..." the man continued, "my son works for the watchman and is in charge of ringing the bell. If you see him, please make sure he's out of harm's way. His name is Jack."

"Jack... ?" echoed Luc.

"Yes. He got the job because we consented to have the fire alarm here at the pharmacy."

"We'll find him," Amelia said. Luc shot her a look.

"Remember, to get across up north, take the La Salle Tunnel back under the river to the city."

"C'mon!" Luc said.

The three young rescuers ran toward the boat. The wind was swirling all around them and constantly changing directions as the fire turned into a weather system of its own. The fire pushed to the northeast and the center of town. The red and orange beast was now in so many places she resembled a blowtorch running unfettered from building to building.

"By now the watchman must see this conflagration," Luc said.

Still, he knew all information was key to the rescue and halting or slowing the fire's path. Luc, Amelia, and Brutus had found the boat amid the trees. Luc struggled with the oars as Amelia and Brutus looked on. Amelia snickered.

"Hey, either one of you want to do this?" Luc said, trying to coordinate strokes.

As they approached the other side of the river, Luc could feel the tug of the currents. "Amelia, are you ready on the bow? When we get close to the pier, tie us off."

"Um, Luc? We don't have any rope."

"Great. Well then, I'll row past the dock and let the current drag us into it. Be ready to jump... Only one chance." Luc rowed with all his strength to get ahead of the pier. It seemed for every pull forward on the oars, in recovery, the boat would fall back.

"Faster, Luc, faster!" shouted Amelia, while Brutus barked. Finally he covered enough ground to position the vessel just north of the pier. Luc and Amelia jumped as the boat sped under the pier southbound. Amelia landed firmly, while Luc was clinging to some planking.

"Whoops, close call." Once Luc regained his footing, he realized Brutus was missing. He looked up to see his expressionless canine companion still in the boat.

"Oh no. Brutus! Jump! Hurry!" Brutus disappeared into the dark. Luc looked to Amelia, who was looking at Brutus as he disappeared. The boat moved swiftly under the pier and downstream, out of sight around a small point of tall tule weeds. The two gathered themselves on the embankment straining their eyes, hoping to see Brutus.

"We need to get to City Hall," Luc finally conceded.

"We can't leave him here." As if out of thin air, Brutus appeared at their feet. Luc and Amelia knelt down to pet him.

"I thought you were lost for sure." Luc said.

Brutus grumble-barked. Then burped.

"He says, 'not a chance,'" Amelia interpreted.

"Oh, so you speak dog now?" pressed Luc.

Brutus bit onto Luc's pants leg and began to pull him forward.

"Okay, okay, we're coming."

With his stubby rear leading the way, Brutus guided them north. Luc pointed. "There it is! The tunnel, La Salle Street Tunnel. Look at all the people running away from the city."

"Doesn't look to be much room for us with everyone coming in our direction," observed Amelia. Luc could see the same thing.

"Now that's fighting the tide," remarked Luc. And beyond in the city, the fire was gaining ground and moving swiftly with the help of the wind and the fuel—all that unused timber—present everywhere.

Luc sized up the scene at the tunnel. Then he noticed Brutus standing aside one of the unused portals, where the pedestrians normally crossed. He could see water breaking through the brick walls, giving way to the river.

"Amelia, I need to get to the courthouse, and this is the only way. I'm sure I can sneak through. Stay here with Brutus, and I'll be back. Okay?"

Amelia stood speechless as Luc ran into the tunnel. As water began to overtake the entrance, Luc sloshed his way to one side with little difficulty. But the other side was filled with panicked people overwhelmed by fear. Amid the noise and confusion, Luc could hear the courthouse bell ringing out, alerting the city to the relentless inferno engulfing Chicago. Then it dawned on him. *The pharmacist's son, Jack!* he thought. *Jack? He must be a relative of Jack's! Oh no...* Luc's rescue now had a greater purpose. Just then his cell rang its alarm. *Not much time.*

Luc ran toward the sound of the bell. He could feel the superheated winds driving embers from the south. The once safer portion of Chicago was now just fuel for the out-of-control blaze. The southerly wind had begun to create its own weather and generate an increasing degree of ferocity. Luc made it to the courthouse just as the bell tower's peaked roof caught fire. He knew from history that the bell would come crashing down and City Hall would be destroyed. It was only a question of when. And Jack had been sent there to ring the bell. As the bell continued to toll, Luc made entry on the north side of the tower.

"Jack, can you hear me?" He tried to shout over the bonging bell. Impossible. Then he realized if he halted the bell by tying off the rope from below, Jack would investigate. On his first attempt, Luc failed and was now moving up and down with the bell. On his next attempt, while on the downswing, Luc made a quick half-hitch and reached for the large brass cleat. *Got it!* As the rope pulled up, Luc was freed.

The weight of the bell and the slack of the rope caused a massive pull of opposite forces. The cleat was almost unhitched from its post.

"Jack, you have to get out of there. I'm Luc. Your father sent me!" Jack could not see from his position that the courthouse was now totally consumed by fire. The smoke had covered any view from above. Just then, the great bell began to give way.

Jack was still unaware of what was happening. He yelled back to Luc. "I can't get down. The belfry timbers are blocking my way."

"You'll have to slide down the bell rope! Now!" Luc shouted. The brass cleat he had tied to the rope gave way with the pressure. The slack rope was now out of reach. As Jack began to slide, Luc strained to grab the end of the rope. Surprisingly, as he took it in his hands and began to control it, he could see the amulet growing closer. Jack continued to descend from the bell tower.

Momentarily letting go of the rope, Luc made an attempt to grab the amulet. Jack began to flail against the inner walls, about to fall to his death, when Luc reengaged. The amulet faded into the smoke.

Jack made his way to the bottom of the rope with Luc standing by. "I had no idea the fire had made it this far into the courthouse," Jack said, bent over and catching his breath.

"Jack, I'm Luc."

"Thank you for..."

"We are so out of here," Luc said, pulling at the other boy. "We got to go—and fast!" Luc gave Jack a two-handed boost out through a ground-floor window leading to the inner courtyard.

"Luc, this isn't out! It's in." With an instantaneous burst of violent energy, the courthouse bell came crashing down with such force no one could have escaped its path. An enormous cloud of dust filled the perimeter of the site.

As Luc and Jack peered out, they turned to each other at the same time and said, "That was..."

"...really close."

They both stopped short, Jack out of surprise, Luc because he remembered that only he and his Jack back home used to finish each other's sentences. But there was no time.

The boys headed out into the streets, where the wooden sidewalks were like lit fuses fueling the fire around them. The winds had intensified from the firestorm, and people were barely escaping the flames. Luc stopped running.

"Jack, we can't outrun this thing. It'll beat us no matter where we go."

"What do you mean? You just saved my life! We can't stop now!"

Luc was already sizing up the options. He could see a stable through the smoke. It was made of brick and wood but was not yet involved in any fire. *Not much can burn,* he thought. Even though the radiant heat was severe and the fire was marching toward them, Luc began to drag Jack into the middle of the ringed exterior corral.

"Okay, here's the plan... We're gonna do a shake and bake."

"What?" Jack looked like he was panicking, breathing too fast, his eyes wide and fearful.

"Jack, trust me. It's the only way. We'll lie down in the path of the fire in a cleaned-out spot on the ground free of anything that can burn."

"Not me."

"You've got to do it. It's the only way. The wind is increasing, and if we time it right, it will blow right over us. Now grab those leather tarps over there, and I'll clear the area."

The fire was bearing down hard and taking everything in its path. Luc looked up to the sky and whispered, "Hope that *Wildland Firefighting* manual knows what it's talking about, Grandpa. This is not a drill."

The two boys got under the tarp. Their only sense of what was happening was the increasing roar of the fire and the pressure they felt as it swarmed over them as if they were being swallowed up. As soon as it seemed it could not get any worse, it was over.

Luc exhaled. "It worked."

"You mean you've never done that before?" Jack asked.

"Well, no." Luc confessed. "But most of it was in the manual I read."

Jack shook his head in disbelief and got a little bit wobbly on his feet. Luc propped him up, his blood still pumping from the excitement. He pointed to the west. "Let's finish this thing. One last gauntlet to safety... getting through the La Salle Tunnel."

Luc and Jack headed toward the tunnel. When they arrived at the entrance, two of the three bores were overcome with river water. The brick portal had caved in with no chance of entry.

"Jack, it looks a bit limited, but let's go for it, what do you say?" Before Jack could even answer, Luc began to drag him toward the last tunnel.

"Third tunnel's the charm." Once again, his smartphone reminded him, time was of the essence. And he remembered Amelia. Was she still safe? With water rushing from all sides of the third bore, and just two small voids, Luc noticed a hand railing.

"Jack, here it is, no biggie. Put this hasty harness around your chest, and we'll hook you into the railing. I can't believe there's actually rope lying around when you need it. C'mon now, I'm right with you." Luc whipped out his belt of webbing and carabiner and hooked in. "It's not so bad except for the spots where the water is sweeping people from their feet."

With headway came more water. Then the boys came up on a rope end flowing with the water's surface. Luc suspected it was being fed to them by Amelia and Brutus—it was too coincidental otherwise. But to access it, they would have to release their stronghold on the railing and just go for the rope. If they could pull themselves along the water's surface, there was about 50 feet to the other end.

Jack began to panic. "Luc, I'm stuck. I can't reach the rope. It won't stay still."

Luc pushed ahead and lunged for the dangling rope. As he secured the rope and Jack, an image began to appear through the rapids. It was the amulet growing closer and closer. But Luc had his hands full with Jack.

"The amulet, Grandpa, what do I do?" Luc muttered in frustration, trying not to gulp down a river of water. His instincts told him to continue to focus on the rescue.

"Don't worry, Jack, I'm here. Give it all you got, and we're home free."

Jack took a deep breath and continued to reach, hand over hand, Luc guiding him from behind. Jack turned to look at Luc, when he heard the strange, fading sound of the ding from Luc's phone. Then he lost sight of Luc.

"Luc, where are you?" Jack had made it to the west side where there was no further danger. All he could see was the collapsing of the La Salle Tunnel into the river. But Jack was on safe ground. He was saved!

Meanwhile, Luc found himself in the clouded conveyor of time travel.

Crash! Bang! Plop! He was back in Grandpa's front room with the dogs, and Amelia was fast asleep on Brutus's heaving belly.

"Grandpa, can we work on these reentries? They're beginning to hurt." Grandpa chuckled as he gave Luc a hug. Grandpa looked and acknowledged the bust of Florian. "Luc, I think we're getting pretty close. Yes, sir, pretty close."

"You were right, Grandpa. Mrs. O'Leary got a bad rap. It wasn't her fault at all." Luc was now looking at the bust.

"Will I ever reach that amulet?"

At that moment Amelia woke up, stretching her arms above her head while Brutus wheeze-burped and stretched his paws. "I just had the most amazing dream..."

Chapter Thirteen

THE NEXT DAY, LUC AND AMELIA SAT ON HER FRONT porch next door to Grandpa's. Luc tried to explain what they had both just experienced. Amelia sat there with a blank expression on her face.

"You don't believe me, do you?"

"Yeah, I sort of believe you. And I totally believe your grandfather. I'm just trying to figure out what it all means."

"Like what?"

"Maybe the amulet isn't a solid, tangible object. Maybe it appears... to guide you?"

"Like a compass, or a beacon..."

"Exactly."

"Hmm. Maybe... Would explain why I can't seem to grab it."

A faint smile crept across the corners of Amelia's mouth. She looked at Luc. Apparently, it was contagious.

"But here's the thing, Luc. Even if you're not totally sure what it is, it's clear that you've been called to duty. You have to keep going after the amulet till you find your answer."

"That's what I've been thinking. What about you?"

"I'm not certain what part I play in this, but it sure is more fun than studying calculus."

"You're studying calculus... during summer vacation?"

"Well, you're saving lives."

Luc started to think he was beginning to like Amelia... maybe... just a little bit. She was kinda cool. "Let's go see what Grandpa has to say."

They climbed the steps up to the grand house, where Luc rang the bell. He tried the front door, but it was locked, and all three dogs were barking.

"Oh, this is his downtown day."

"What?" Amelia said.

Luc explained that once a week Grandpa would jump on a streetcar and make his way around the city, reminiscing about the great old days in San Francisco and getting some fresh air. But Grandpa was a very punctual man and always home by 4:05 P.M.—always. Luc checked his cell.

"We're way early. He won't be home for another 45 minutes."

"You want to wait at my house? It's kinda cold out here."

"Nah, we can go in. Grandpa won't mind."

"By breaking and entering?"

"No, silly, we'll use the doggie door. I've done it a hundred times." Luc walked to the back of the house with Amelia tagging along. He attempted to assist Amelia over the fence, but she had already scaled it with ease, leaving him in the dust. Luc shook his head and then crawled over the top. No luck. Another inside door, which was closed and locked, blocked the doggie door.

"No biggie, there's always a window." Luc looked up the driveway from side to side.

"Oh, I know! Wait here." He then proceeded to shimmy up the rainspout, jiggling a window ajar and then opening it.

"It's not breaking and entering..." he shouted down. "It's forcible entry."

But Amelia was gone. Luc made his way down the stairs only to find Renzo, Dante, Brutus, and Amelia at the foot of the stairs.

"How did you get in?"

"Somebody unlocked the door."

Brutus barked. "Okay, wonderdog. Just make sure you know who it is before—" Luc stopped himself. "Okay, this is ridiculous. That dog can't do that. Forget it, we're in."

The two made their way into the adjoining room. "I love to poke around Grandpa's house. Everything has a story behind it."

Despite the fact that they had both been in the living room many times, somehow it felt awkward without Grandpa. Still, there was a sense of excitement connected to their snooping. They fixed their eyes on every small artifact from Grandpa's past, including the aged, leatherbound journals from eras gone by. There were paintings and models of stately old ships, firehouse clocks, crystals, piles of scrolled maps, and busts of who knows whom. And along with the vintage, ornate furniture in perfect condition, there was a jewel-encrusted table. Grandpa's living room was a treasure trove of cool things.

As Luc and Amelia walked about the room in different directions, they studied each item knowing there was a story behind every piece. Eventually they met in front of the most compelling and entrancing feature in the room, the bust of Florian, the Roman fire-fighter and soldier. There, next to Florian was a framed, aged picture of a beautiful woman holding a musical instrument. She stood by the railing on board a large ship, against the backdrop of an expansive ocean. Luc picked up the photo of his grandmother with wonder, at the same time, as if in sync, the teens drew from their focus and found themselves gazing at the bust of Florian. The carved marble eyes seemed to come alive with a hypnotic depth, taking them both in.

At that moment, they both snapped out of their apparent trance.

"Was that statue looking at us?" Amelia shivered at the creepiness.

"Yeah! Did you see that, too?" Luc said. They both turned back to the statue.

"Luc, I think Florian is talking to us."

Luc's attention was drawn to Brutus's sniveling and grunting.

"Amelia, forget that. We've got other problems." Luc pointed to Grandma's squeezebox in full exhalation, swaying on the rocker, as the Greek fire sparked in the hearth. "No dreaming going on here."

"Grandpa's not here. No story, no background, no path!"

"Luc, put the helmet on. It must be time."

Luc reached for Lucky Leather and began to put it on, then stopped short. "Maybe it's wrong without Grandpa here."

"Luc, someone needs you!" Amelia pleaded.

"You believe in all this, don't you?"

"Yes, yes I believe. Are you going or what?"

"Not yet. I think I should wait for Grandpa. He never tells me what to do, but he always kinda gives me a pep talk or story beforehand."

"Hey, dude, does this mean we're officially friends?"

That was random of her, Luc thought. He opted for sarcastic. "Like BFFs? That's for girls."

"Softball pitchers don't *do* the BFF thing. We're more like... teammates then, right?"

Luc nodded. "Yeah. Teammates."

Luc placed the fireworn leather helmet back on the mantle. The squeezebox ceased to circulate, and the Greek fire returned to a soft glow amid the embers. As the large firehouse clock struck 16:00 hours, or 4:00 P.M. to civilians, Grandpa entered the room with a big smile, appearing not at all surprised to see his two young guests.

"Good to see you two! Ah yes, and you, too, Brutus." The dogs rallied and woofed around him.

"Sorry we barged in like this, Grandpa."

"Yeah, we're sorry, Captain Sullivan."

"Never a problem, son. And you're always welcome here, Amelia."

Evidently Grandpa was unfazed by how they got inside the house. Luc put the picture of Grandma back in its place. Grandpa reached over Luc's shoulder and adjusted the position of the frame. He put a hand on Luc's shoulder. "I can see a lot of her in you, Luc. I wish you could have known her better."

"Me, too."

"Captain Sullivan, can you tell me more about Mrs. Sullivan. She's so beautiful."

Luc surrendered to the moment. And anyway, anytime was a good time to listen to one of Grandpa's stories. He and Amelia sat on the rug in front of Grandpa, who was on the couch. They both kept an eye on the bust of Florian directly over his shoulder.

"I met Mrs. Sullivan, Luc's grandmother, in 1903 while sailing aboard the Kaiser Wilhelm II—*The Ocean*

Greyhound as they called her, sailing from Bantry Bay, where I had been visiting my own mother." Grandpa reached for a photo album on top of the end table, and motioned to the teens to come over. They both got on their knees as he propped the album on his lap. He opened the album to a picture of the steamship.

"Built in 1897, she was 700 feet long and weighed 31 tons..." And although Luc and Amelia were not time traveling presently, Grandpa was such an excellent storyteller they felt like they were there on the ship with him.

"She had twin propellers, and two four-cylinder, triple-expansion reciprocating steam engines. The vessel was often covered in fog, and there were always people milling about the deck, both night and day." Grandpa turned the page of the album, revealing a picture of him in his mid-twenties.

"You look like Dad."

"And very handsome," added Amelia. "I just love a good romance!"

Luc rolled his eyes.

"How did you meet her?" Amelia asked.

"Well, one evening I was taking a stroll when I heard music spilling from the quarterdeck. A small, makeshift band played while people danced in the center of a gathering crowd. Although the air was foggy and cold, the travelers seemed joyous as they celebrated the voyage taking them from the Old Sod to a New Land.

"I moved around so I could get a better view of the rousing jig that was taking place. Then I saw her—a radiant young woman playing a squeezebox. She caught me staring at her and offered a faint smile. I scanned the area for a deck chair, and then I brought it to her side and introduced myself.

"My name is Captain Con Sullivan. Ma'am, may I offer you a chair?"

"Well, Conny, I thank you. But where were you twenty minutes ago? My dogs were beat already then."

"Ah, better late than never. And before you batter me down much more, may I ask the name of my assailant and player of such grand music?"

"I'll think about it. So Conny..."

"Please call me Con."

"Okay. So Conny, why haven't I seen you before this evening? We've been out in the Atlantic floating around for days, and now out of the fog you show up with a chair? I could have used this days ago."

"My error. Should have been sooner. Would I have already received your name if I had come earlier?"

"Possibly, just possibly."

"May I escort you to your quarters?"

"That's a bit forward of you."

"Just trying to be a gentleman. Can I carry your accordion?"

"It's a squeezebox, Conny."

I reached for the instrument, but she yanked it away.

"No, I'll take care of this myself. Nice to meet you, Mister? Captain? Of what? Sullivan." She started to walk away, but turned her head over her shoulder, flinging her hair back, flirting with me mercilessly and saying... "Theresa Gallagher is my name."

"And that's how it all started."

"Did Grandma have these powers?" Luc asked.

"These powers you speak of were a blessing from our Celtic past, dating back to a time before Catholicism and Christianity. These ancient ways were only to be used for the good of all. In order to work, they needed to be in the hands of the right man."

"Or woman," Amelia interjected.

"That's right, Amelia. For it was Mrs. Sullivan who introduced them to me."

Luc turned toward the rocker. "That's why Grandma was so protective of the squeezebox!"

"Till she got to know me," boasted Grandpa. He placed the photo album back on the table. Amelia was looking at Theresa's picture in the frame next to Florian.

"There's a reason your grandma's picture sits next to Florian there on the mantle. Luc, your ancestors were proud Celtic people, a people who had vast influence all over Europe, not just in Ireland. The people of Enns, Austria, were also of Celtic heritage."

"Isn't that where Florian was stationed?"

"Yes, my boy, good memory! Also where he gave his life while protecting others."

"Like firefighters," Amelia said.

"Like firefighters," Grandpa agreed. "Grandma Theresa was proud of her Celtic heritage and felt a special connection to Florian and his legacy." As the three stood in front of the framed photo, Florian's eyes seemed like they were coming to life once again.

"Grandpa, do you see that?"

"Creepy." Amelia frowned.

"But not dangerous or demonic. He's a protector, after all. You're connected to him too, Luc. Just like your grandmother."

The bellows of the squeezebox began to breathe again, and the fire sparked and popped once more, gaining in luminescence. Grandpa had his hands on both Luc's and Amelia's shoulders, while Luc donned Lucky Leather—this time with renewed confidence. Then... Crash! Bang! Plop!

Chapter Fourteen

THE TRIP WAS FASTER THIS TIME AS THEY HARDLY noticed the conveyor, but the landing was abrupt, and Luc, Amelia, and Brutus all piled onto each other.

This time they were covered in a thick layer of dust. As they pulled themselves upright and brushed off the dust, they realized they had landed in what looked to be a quarry, complete with large, unfinished statues. Luc turned around and came face to face with a full-sized sculpture of Florian. Then they felt the vibration of a growing thunder advancing their way. A cloud of dust was attached to the sound, and it was roaring in their direction. As it got closer you could see a team of horses leading what looked like a chariot with two riders.

"They look like Roman soldiers," noted Amelia. The two friends looked around and saw an ancient city that somehow looked brand new. Luc began to unscramble things.

"Florian... I think we're here in Enns, Austria. Amelia, we've got to get to Florian before it's too late! This rescue has to happen." Not thinking of the course of history, he grabbed Amelia by the hand and began the quest.

As they entered the town square, an eerie feeling of desolation overcame them. There were no people anywhere. But a large smoldering fire enveloped a giant, scorched cross. Brutus began to whine. From out of nowhere they heard someone beckoning them.

"Psst, psst, over here." A small, elderly, fragile-looking man waved them over from behind the stone wall.

"You must get off the streets. It isn't safe. They are killing people."

"Who are they killing?" Luc asked.

"Florian, the protector. They failed to burn him alive. Now they mete their violence on the Christians, raiding their homes and murdering even their children."

"Where is Florian now?" Amelia said.

"They have dragged him away in chains. They plan to drown him in the river."

Luc looked around for transportation, but quickly remembered where he was. "Which way, man?"

"He means 'sir,'" Amelia interjected. She wanted to kick Luc.

"The road goes around the river. Go over the top of the ridge to the trail. It is steep but quicker than the road."

The old man was staring at their clothes—and especially Brutus. "Godspeed, my young, strange friends." Brutus barked. "And you as well, whatever you are, strange beast."

Luc and Amelia clawed up the steep terrain and onto the trail, ignoring the scrapes and abrasions they received from the rough terrain. They reached a point where they could see a crowd of mostly soldiers gathered below. Amelia spotted a man in shackles who appeared to be Florian standing on the embankment of the Enns River. Amelia pointed in his direction. "That's him, right there."

The soldiers began to chain a huge millstone around his neck. The decree rang out in the canyon so all could hear. "This Florian, this traitor, stands accused of insubordination, treason, witchcraft, and Christianity."

"Witchcraft?" said Luc.

"Yes, they can't believe he escaped the execution by fire without some help from a 'demon within.' I saw a special about it on the History Channel," Amelia said.

Luc shook his head. Was there nothing this girl did not know?

A fight of some type ensued below, with supporters of Florian trying to remove the stone around his neck and the soldiers yanking them back, with one even plunging a sword into a man who had Florian by the waist. Luc knew that now was the time to make a move. The crowd grew in numbers, as it seemed the whole town was gathering. Amelia looked to see Luc on his cell as they made their way downstream.

"What are you doing?"

"Calm down! I'm checking the swift water rescue app on my phone. Can't lose your cool, okay?"

"Okay."

"Okay, here's the deal. Need some rope, a couple of long poles, and horses. I've got my webbing belt and carabiners."

"We're on it." Amelia said." "C'mon, Brutus."

Knowing that the furious river was Florian's fate, Luc began to study the water for entry and the best place to traverse the current so he could intercept Florian. Amelia and Brutus returned with all the supplies.

"Where did you get all that?"

"Someone left a chariot parked around the bend," Amelia answered as she took the rope from Brutus's mouth and placed spears in the ground.

"Wow... I'm impressed!" It was her turn to look at him smugly. "Really, why? 'Cause I'm a girl?" She was straight-faced then suddenly smiled.

Luc could feel his face flushing. She was definitely not one of the guys. But there was no time to get weird right now.

Brutus began to drag the rest of the supply cache forward, a bounty that included leather straps, blankets, and even two swords.

"Wow, you got a ton of stuff." Then Luc heard whinnies and snorts coming over the crest and turned to see Brutus leading a couple of horses with their reins in his mouth. Luc's phone alarm sounded.

"Dang! We gotta hurry!"

At that moment a loud murmur rose in cadence from the edge of the crowd into a huge roar below. A man sprang forward from the mob and leveraged the millstone around Florian's neck over the embankment. As the slack of the rope uncoiled, a loop in the excess lassoed a child at his feet and catapulted him into the river, Florian following close behind.

"Secure the end of this rope to the chariot. It's zip-line time! And pack the net on my back for the boy. Welcome to the fire service, Amelia. We'll catch Florian as he moves downstream. And give me a couple of spears, too."

Amelia took speedy action without hesitation. Luc immediately configured a running bowline over his shoulder and under his arm, safety checking connections, now fastened. Realizing the weight would sink at some point, he descended into as shallow water as possible before beginning to traverse the rapids. The water was moving swiftly, and Luc aggressively crawled perpendicular to the ferocious white waves. With little time on top, he made it to an eddy behind a protruding boulder, center stream. Luc took a huge gulp of air and swam to the bottom, slogging through the calm water below. Then he surfaced behind the boulder and created a space, or purchase as they called it, behind the rock. Luc spotted the boy holding tightly to a tree branch extended over the water near the shore. Florian was pulled along the bottom by the raging current. But Luc knew that the millstone around Florian's neck would get caught at some point. Quick decision... while the boy was momentarily safe, he would try to save Florian.

Luc prepared the net as well as the spears that would be used for stability. His webbing and carabiner belt were configured to what was called a lark's foot that was anchored to a point on the boulder. Amelia looked on and recognized that the prep work was complete. She took up the slack rope when Luc gave her the signal. He gave her a thumbs-up and moved on to the next task.

Luc climbed to a spot on the boulder to try and get a glimpse of Florian, while the boy continued to cling to the unreliable branch. Once atop, Brutus was there, barking uncontrollably. Luc realized that Brutus had spotted the millstone and its path as it flowed toward them.

"You deserve a cookie later, Brutus." As the stone tumbled below the current, drawing closer, Luc could see a green blur just below the surface.

"The amulet!" The millstone dragging Florian became entrapped by Luc's net. Luc dived into the deep water with his Leatherman knife in his teeth. Descending into the cold, dark Alpine water, he saw a bright green light emanating from the amulet. The millstone had transformed. Luc could now see Florian, and Luc swam as fast as he could to reach his hero. Gasping for air, now face to face with this firefighter soldier, Luc saw Florian open his eyes. As the two made eye contact, it was clear they both clearly understood what was at stake. So with precious little time left, Florian spoke under the water.

"The boy..." he said, and then went unconscious.

Luc hesitated only for a second. But his hero was already on his way to meeting his fate. This was a part of history that could not be changed. Luc let go and swam swiftly toward the boy, who was now holding onto the tree branch with his fingertips. He swept the boy up in his arms as Brutus began to bark, signaling Amelia to have the horses pull.

As the rescue began, Luc could see the green light from the amulet sinking further and further into the deep, then disappearing. Instantly, the river became completely calm, like a mirror with small ripples vibrating from Luc's phone. The conveyor had begun, and it was time to go. Luc lifted the boy to the shore, where the child was gathered up by the crowd. As the compatriots began to tumble through time, all Luc could see were the eyes of his hero, Florian. Opened, to acknowledge a fellow rescuer, a fellow soldier. Then fading closed as he sank to the bottom.

Then... Crash! Bang! Plop!

Chapter Fifteen

Luc FOUND HIMSELF ON GRANDPA'S LIVING ROOM rug, with his dad standing behind Grandpa, who was seated in his chair. Amelia had somehow reentered in a standing position, flanked by Brutus, and was holding onto what appeared to be a Roman centurion's helmet.

"Oh!" she exclaimed, while the others looked on. "I saw it in the chariot and just wanted to try it on."

And with that it disappeared. They all looked at each other. Amelia spoke first. "Okay, weirdness. Moving on now?"

"Dad..." Luc began, "Florian, the amulet..."

"It's all right, Luc," Grandpa reassured him, standing to his full height. "The amulet is part of you. Your spirit to protect and rescue when needed is all that's required."

"The amulet as you understand it will be there when you need it," his dad said.

"Well that's good, 'cause I'm in. All the way. How about you, Ameila?"

"You bet!" Amelia said, giving Luc a harmless sidelong glance that made him want to crawl under the rug. Girls were so weird.

"Right this way, you two." They followed Grandpa, entering the dining room. To Luc's surprise, the table was fully set for dinner—for five. Mom entered from the kitchen with a big platter of roast beef and a smile from ear to ear.

"Wash your hands, you two. I'm sure you've covered a lot of territory."

Luc and Amelia moved to the double kitchen sink and began to soap up.

"Well, that was kind of awesome," Amelia whispered.

Luc grinned from one corner of his mouth. "All in a day's work, Amelia." *Was that cool of me to say or dorky?* he wondered.

Mom rang a small bell in the other room, and with that Dante and Renzo tore into the dining room only to find Brutus already licking his chops from a morsel that had "fallen" on the floor.

Everyone sat down with Grandpa at the head of the table. Grandpa looked at all of them and beamed with pride as he folded his hands and bowed his head for a quiet blessing. After a moment he announced, "Let's eat!" As he began to pass the platter of food, Luc's mom addressed her son.

"Luc, football game tomorrow so... good dinner, the dishes, and a good night's sleep."

"Dishes?"

"No slacking 'round here. You've got the watch, my boy," Mom said in her commanding voice. But she said it with an amazing smile. That's how she always got Luc to do things. And as Luc would soon come to learn, that was pretty much how all females got their men to do what they wanted. A little sugar would even get a rescue hero to finish mending a fence.

Chapter Sixteen

AFTER DINNER GRANDPA, MRS. SULLIVAN, AND Amelia sat sipping hot chocolate and chatting in the living room, while Renzo and Dante snored near their feet. Luc and his dad were sitting outside on the front steps with Brutus.

"How do you feel, son?"

"Like I've got lots of energy. And kinda disappointed."

"By what?"

"I knew that Florian's choice was also his destiny, but I still feel responsible."

"I understand. Trying to save a life is an incredibly difficult thing to do. And it's even harder when you fail."

Luc could see a glint of pain left in his dad's eyes. He put his arm on Captain Sullivan's shoulder. "I get it. But Dad... wasn't I supposed to retrieve the amulet and return it to its rightful place to make things right and save the family history?"

"You did, Luc. The amulet lies in the deep with Florian. But it also resides with us."

"You mean like a symbol."

"Go check out Florian's bust."

Luc made his way into the front room. He reached for the bust of Florian, lifting it up for the first time, feeling its heft—and feeling a long chain slide out of the back from a hidden cavern behind the bust. He let the entire chain out, running it through his fingers till he reached a bump. He turned the bust around. There lay an emerald green stone set in a casing of gold. He looked up at his dad who had come in and stood behind him.

"What? Where'd it come from? What does it mean?"

"It means it's home... until your next dispatch, rookie."

CPSIA information can be obtained
at www.ICGtesting.com
Printed in the USA
FSOW02n2120250216
17156FS